Pressure Point

How beautiful it must have been, she thought, to sit before a fire here and watch it flicker on the wide mantelpiece. Or maybe she'd have an orchestra in and have a dance. She would throw a huge ball and dance all night. Imagining herself dressed in a dazzling gown, she lifted her arms to embrace an invisible partner and whirled about in the first step of a waltz.

As she turned, her song choked to a terrified stop in her throat. There stood the ugliest little man she had ever seen. He was pointing a gun at her.

"Don't move," he said. "And don't make a sound. Leave your hands up."

Her whole body went rigid as he searched her, touching her all over, the sickening odor of stale cigarettes and coffee hot in her face. Her stomach heaved with fear and the utter shock of what was happening to her.

"All right," he said. "Walk in front of me." And he jammed the point of the pistol in her back.

**Other Point™ paperbacks
you will enjoy:**

Last Seen on Hopper's Lane

Janet Allais Stegeman

SCHOLASTIC INC.
New York Toronto London Auckland Sydney

ISBN 0-590-33108-6

Copyright © 1982 by Janet Allais Stegeman. All rights reserved. Published by Scholastic Inc., 730 Broadway, New York, NY 10003, by arrangement with Dial Books for Young Readers, a division of E.P. Dutton, Inc.

12 11 10 9 8 7 6 5 4 3 2 1   12   5 6 7 8 9/8 0/9

For Zachary and Laura

Acknowledgments

My thanks go to Detective Joel M. Casper, Criminal Investigation Division; Corporal Mel Hegwood, Public Information Officer, of the Police Department, Athens, Georgia, and to staff members of the Northeast Georgia Police Academy, University of Georgia.

I am also indebted to Akins Ford, Winder, Georgia, and Trussell Ford-Mazda, Athens, Georgia.

Many readers made suggestions along the way that proved invaluable to the clarity and direction of this story. One must be singled out: Mary Anne Hodgson, whose willing, capable, and fearless blue pencil went over the final drafts.

To my husband, Dr. John F. Stegeman, I am deeply grateful, for without his patient help this book would not have been possible.

1

The dark green van entered the northbound freeway carefully. It held the right-hand lane, then fed into the traffic heading through Georgia.

Carl's hands had begun to sweat. He was scared now that they were actually nearing the drop-off place. This was only his second job, the first time he'd been sent out with Ax, and getting rid of the stuff was just as risky as picking it up; there was always the chance that something would go wrong.

From the corner of his eye he could see Ax's profile hunched over the steering wheel—the heavy jaw, the eyebrows that met in a perpetual scowl over a beak of a nose. The man must have known Carl was looking because he turned toward him and Carl saw the jagged edge of the scar that gave him the nickname Ax. Carl would have called him Ax without the scar, but, as if by punctuation, there had been a long-ago fight and the man's face had been laid open by a heavy blade. Now it was a puckered road through the stubble of beard. Ugly.

Carl turned away and looked down at the map in his lap. He had been looking at it for so many hours it had begun to blur. His mind was full of questions he was forbidden to ask. He had no idea how big the total operation was except what he had pieced together from snatches of conversation he was not supposed to have heard. He could only guess the rest. And he guessed he had stumbled onto something big. Otherwise why all the different license plates he had to change every eighty miles, and the cans of spray paint in the back to change the color of the van when Ax ordered him to? The tag on the van right now said Minnesota, but that didn't mean a thing. There were forty other tags in a box in back. And he didn't even know the driver's real name. That was part of it—part of the whole setup. That way nobody could tell anybody anything. Not a thing. Because nobody knew anything to tell.

At least, that's what they thought. Now Carl wondered if Ax suspected how much he had overheard. Ax had come unexpectedly out of the shadows at the old dock near Darien where Carl had been instructed to go to pick up this second haul. Carl had gone there because after what they had done to Dinghy he was afraid not to go.

He had waited in the dark on the old dock, not knowing what to expect, not knowing exactly what was going on, feeling panic rise. It was there he overheard the low voices coming from one of the shrimp boats that wallowed in the narrow tidewater between the marsh grasses and the dock.

The small ugly man had been standing there, nearly invisible, for some time before Carl saw him. In the darkness, with only a thin moon for light, Carl felt the skin on the back of his neck move. This man, Ax, was to be his new partner. Carl knew from the moment he saw him that working with Ax would not be the kind of dumb fun he and Dinghy had gone in for. This small, ugly man reduced Carl's own hugeness to nothing. And he was afraid.

Behind the seats of the van were mounds that looked like laundry bundles. Carl turned to check them, tucked in a flap of the tarpaulin covering them more snugly, then looked at his map once more. He watched the uniform green road signs go by, gauging the miles by the map. His head had begun to ache hours ago, the way it had when he was a little kid and got carsick in his uncle's truck. It was his tension and fear mixed with the nauseating fumes from the cans of extra gas they carried.

He swallowed the nausea. "Should be the fourth exit up."

Ax nodded.

"Jesus," Carl said and tried to keep his young male voice from cracking, "I'll be glad to get this stuff stowed."

The man beside him was silent.

"Well, I sure as hell hope you know where we're going," Carl said. "Because there isn't a thing marked on this map about any old house in Blanton, Georgia."

Ax looked at him with icy contempt. "Of course there isn't."

"Well, do you know?"

"I know."

"Is it safe?"

Ax didn't answer. He was busy checking the side mirror to see if anyone was following.

2

The old deserted stone mansion pleased Kerry most from this view. She had discovered the place by chance when she was looking for a short cut from Johnson Drive through to Dexter Street. She figured that this narrow, overgrown dirt road, remote and rutted as it was, saved her about two miles from her high school to home on the edge of town. After practicing basketball all afternoon, she was tired enough to want to shorten the long bike ride. And the enormous house took her mind off of all the things she didn't want to think about.

There was a grassy hump under a big yellow poplar on the low bank opposite the estate where she liked to sit and rest before plugging up the steep incline to Dexter. It was from this vantage point that the house most fascinated her. She had made up a game about it. From here, looking up to where it stood on the crest of Hopper's Hill, she never thought of it as deserted and falling to ruin. It looked solid, as if in a moment, when the sun set completely, lights would come on in the long mullioned windows, and maybe, even though it was warm for a mid-October day, smoke would curl from the four enormous stone chimneys.

In her game she owned the estate. She made mental notes of how she would restore the place.

First she would do something about this lane that served as access road.

Next, she would fix the long tree-lined driveway to the house. It was badly washed out and there were mimosa and pine seedlings shooting up, not only there, but all over what once must have been a beautiful lawn. To the right of the house, set off by a row of shrubs gone wild now with neglect, was a sort of summerhouse, a latticed affair whose side wall was bowed out of shape by thick wisteria vines. And the gate—she would try to match the remaining half of the heavy wrought iron so that once again the house could be closed off and protected from passersby.

Suddenly Kerry realized the sun had sunk lower. Should she wait any longer? It was getting late. Maybe he wasn't coming.

A cold dampness started up from the thick grass where she was sitting, seeping through the seat of her jeans, clammy and unpleasant. She stood up and brushed her jeans off, looking at the glowing sky reflected on the slate roof of the old mansion, on the trunks of the trees lining the long, curving drive.

Everything was tinged an unreal pink. The color was unbelievable, as if someone had poured a jar of raspberry jam over the whole hill. It smeared the roof, caught the windows so that the house looked as if it really were all lit up. Kerry longed for a peek inside but had never dared take much time to rest as she passed. It was always late when she got this far, and she was afraid her mother would worry if she stayed long enough for a real look around.

Maybe this weekend, she thought. Maybe then there will be time, and who knows? There might even be a way to get inside.

She sat down again. "I'll give him one more minute," she told herself. "Then I have to go home."

Jeff Andrews felt the strain as he pounded doggedly on to the crest of the hill. He wondered if he would ever get back in shape. The doctors had warned him that after a broken leg it would take some time, especially with as bad a break as he'd had. He'd only been allowed to try a jog-walk program for the past couple of weeks, and he was disgusted to find that he reached the top of Dexter panting and blowing like an old man instead of the near eighteen-year-old he was. He glanced at his watch. Well, at least his time was getting better. But the ache in his chest, the thudding of his heart, the pain and rubbery feeling in his legs were not what he'd hoped for at this stage of his recovery.

The sky grew red as he turned off the main drag into Hopper's Lane. Would she have waited for him? It was late, he knew. He had come as fast as he could, and this was the farthest he'd tried to go at that pace.

He slowed to a limping walk, glad for the excuse to take it easy on the uneven ground of the lane. He didn't like this lane. There was something about its utter isolation, its obvious lack of regular use that made him uneasy. What he really didn't like was that Kerry always beat him here on her bike and had to wait all by herself.

Then he saw her. She was sitting on her little hump of grass opposite the old house, just staring up at it. He stopped a minute to catch his breath. She *had* waited. It was late, but there she was. It made him feel good. But it made him feel nervous and uncomfortable too. What if something should happen to her way out here?

He remembered the first time he had ever seen her. It was just after school had started back in September. He had hobbled down toward the track next to the practice field, drawn there because he felt miserable and out of things. The doctors had told him that another operation on his leg was a probability. He'd only been off crutches a little over three weeks, and here they were talking about another operation! He knew his place on the track team was shot, but what would that do to his chances of being accepted into the Blanton police cadet program?

The track and practice field were near the courts, and he watched some kids dribbling a basketball around, hooking shots, some others batting a tennis ball. He stared jealously down toward the track where several groups were doing laps and wind sprints. Lord, it had been a long time since he'd run that thing!

And then he saw her, a long-legged girl moving with easy grace up the bank toward the courts. She must have just finished running. Her face was flushed, her bouncy brown hair held off her sticky forehead by a rubber band that was coming loose. As she passed him he saw a little blue clip-thing, a sort of butterfly he guessed, and it was hanging all cockeyed, as if it were about to fall off the rubber band it was supposed to be covering.

Jeff remembered that he was looking for a place to sit down and prop up his leg when a basketball rolled just past him. He started a slow, careful turn to retrieve it, always afraid he would twist something and then they *would* have to operate.

But somebody yelled, "Hey, Kerry! Toss it back, okay?"

The leggy girl with the shiny brown hair snagged the ball, and with a shy grin moved toward the court and banked a beautiful shot off the boards and through the hoop. There was a chorus of cheers. Then with the same graceful lope she trotted off toward the bike stands.

"Who's the basketball star?" Jeff asked.

"You mean Kerry? New kid on the girls' varsity. Transfer from Eastside High," Dave Woods answered.

"Blake," Phil Clark had added. "Kerry Blake."

And from there Jeff had spent a great deal of time finding out more about her.

Now she was waiting for him out here on this godforsaken lane.

He called, "Hey, Kerry!"

She jumped, and he realized that she had been completely absorbed in that old Hopper place. But she waved back and he walked a little faster, rubber legs and all.

She was standing now by the tree where she had propped her ten-speed and he looked again at her slim, leggy build, with a nice pair of shoulders under the sweatshirt. Her hair looked almost red in the setting sun. It had come a little loose from the rubber band's butterfly clip and was curling over part of her forehead.

"I thought you forgot," she said with that shy grin he liked, "or lost your way."

Jeff dropped down on the knoll. "Got a late start and it took me a lot longer than I figured."

"How's the leg?"

"Sore. But I'm working at it. I'm glad you waited."

"I'm glad you came! I was just about to leave. I don't like to make Mom worry."

"I'll just have to start earlier next time, won't I?" He squinted up at her. "You sure were giving that old house the eye. What's up there anyhow?"

"Who knows? I just kind of discovered the neat old place. Dad would have loved it." Her face was reddish, but he couldn't tell whether she was blushing or whether the sunset caused it. "There wasn't anything like this where we used to live. Plenty of nice neighborhoods and all, but, well, this is sort of—"

She stopped and he knew now that she was blushing.

"Romantic," he said and laughed.

"Well—yes."

"This happens to be a deserted part of town, Kerry. I don't know if it's such a hot idea for you to come this way by yourself. And I can't always make it."

She looked surprised. "Nobody's ever out here. And the lane isn't all that long. I mean, there's Johnson Drive not much more than half a mile that way, and Dexter up the hill and around that curve. And it sure saves me time getting home."

"And you sure like that old house," he teased.

"I really do. I'd love to look in the windows some time."

She steered her bike away from its prop against the yellow poplar and straddled it, balancing on her right foot. He stood up, feeling the strain but not wanting it to show.

"I wish you didn't have to go so soon."

"It's—well, I told you all that, Jeff. It's been hard on Mom and she doesn't need to worry about me."

She had told him a great deal in the time they had known each other. Much, and not much. At least, not as much as he would have liked to know. She didn't seem to have made many friends on this side of town or at school. She was shy, sure, but she held a lot back. A sort of loner, he thought, but he didn't care, and he sure liked her.

"I'll call you, okay?" he said.

The crinkly-nose smile. The shy little lift of her mouth as she nodded. "Oh, Kerry," he thought, "you are a very great girl. But getting anywhere with you is just about as hard as getting this leg back in shape!"

"See you," she said, and he watched her wheel the bike over the ruts until she could safely ride it.

Kerry and her bike. A soft fleece-covered narrow seat with the canvas pack behind, reflector tape in the wheels, reflectors on the pedals, a big headlight. All equipped for night riding, but she probably never rode at night. Too afraid her mother would worry. Well, he liked her mother, too, but he wondered if maybe Kerry wasn't losing something by being such a good little daughter.

"No," he thought. "That is exactly why you like her, and you know it. Because she *is* a good kid. Okay, so she doesn't think you're Prince Charming. But she thinks you are a friend. Don't push your luck."

He looked again at the old Hopper House. Well, just what *was* it up there that had to be so all-fired unusual that she'd sit on the cold ground and just stare? Nothing. Just a huge heap of a deserted place. He'd seen it lots of times, but it sure didn't grab him the way it did her. It was one of the last of the big old estates that had dominated this side of town. A few of the old mansions had been torn down to make room for low-rent housing; some had been made into apartments, another the clubhouse for the municipal golf course. But this was a big old rambly barn of a place, with a double-story main part and two huge wings going off at an angle at the sides. It must have looked like a blunted V from the air. And the whole thing shrouded in ivy. Just plain gloomy.

He thought of the times he'd walked over to Kerry's

apartment. His excuse was building up his leg, and he only lived a couple of miles away. When her mother wasn't home, there was never an invitation to come inside. They sat on the steps outside, and Kerry brought out glasses of ice water. Sometimes a Coke. All very old-fashioned and proper. So why should she be hanging around a remote place like this? He walked on slowly, thinking.

All right, so she was hard to get to know. But he hadn't opened up with her completely either. He had not told her that his lifelong ambition was to be a cop, that he had applied for the Blanton police cadet program. How could he tell her that he was really worried that his leg had set him back, because there was a long list of applicants waiting to be processed and accepted? What chance did he have, anyway? He wouldn't even be eighteen for four more months.

Some of the other applicants had already started riding in patrol cars. Some had even been used in routine police work. But he hadn't. Lots of the kids, he realized, had pull—family connections on the force—or had been active in scouting or other things that gave them priority ratings and good character references. Well, he'd tried a lot of those programs, too, but nothing had worked out very well. So he had just given up on it all and taken a job at the car wash on weekends. He wanted to get a car of his own so he wouldn't have to beg old stingy brother John for his. That plan fell through when he broke his leg.

So what did he have going for him? Just that he

wanted very much to be a cop. He always had. He always would. And he had not told Kerry. If he confided all that and nothing came of it, if he were turned down—well, the humiliation would be almost worse than the total, disastrous disappointment he would feel.

Up the lane, at the end that opened into Johnson Drive, he saw a dark green van approaching, and he edged to the side to let it pass. There were two men in it, and he was just as glad he would soon be turning into the main thoroughfare from which they came, especially since it was getting dark.

As the van passed, curiosity made him glance back for a better look. It had a Minnesota tag. They were a long way from home on this deserted lane in Blanton, Georgia. They had probably missed the detour to the north bypass. The access road to it wasn't finished yet, and a lot of out-of-town cars had trouble because the detour was so badly marked. But this was a strange place to end up. He hesitated, thinking maybe he should holler at them. Then he decided against it. He had read of too many innocent people getting mugged for doing just that. They could go on through to Dexter where there was a service station not far off and in plain view.

Puff, puff, gasp. Damn, he was out of shape! He took a deep breath and trotted on.

Mrs. Bertha Murdoch turned left onto Johnson Drive, then slowed down because it was getting dark and she was afraid she would miss the turn into Hopper's Lane. The marker was long gone, to vandals, no doubt. The car crept along. She was aware of the impatience of the drivers behind her, but that could not be helped.

There it was. As she eased the car into the rutted lane the sweep of her headlights flashed on a jogger, who jumped to the side of the road. She slammed on the brakes. The near miss had jangled her already taut nerves, and she clasped the wheel with trembling hands. "Why," she thought, "*why* isn't there a law against all those people running about the streets half-naked and not even looking where they are going?"

It had been a bad day altogether. The city council meeting had dragged on until there was no hope of getting a proper hearing for her committee's project. The report she had worked months on, carefully documenting the need for an arts center for senior citizens, had fallen on a bunch of very deaf ears. She might as well have been talking to a wall. The only council member who had looked the least bit interested was that young Allen Davidson, but he was not on the finance committee and, worse, he wasn't even from her ward. She felt as if the gavel blow had been directed at her when the mayor perfunctorily dismissed her report. "Referred to the finance committee," he had intoned. Then *blam* went the gavel, and that was that.

She and her committee had hoped to get matching funds from the city to go with a grant to procure a place for the older citizens. They had looked at all the available sites, and it did seem to her that they had a very valid argument in favor of buying the old Hopper House. It certainly would cost less to purchase and refurbish than to erect an entirely new building. There was not another place so basically sound, so well situated in quiet surroundings, so perfectly suited to her group's purposes. If only the council had listened. She had presented everything—*everything*! How could they argue with a professional architect's opinion that the place was as solid as a rock and only needed a fourth again as much money beyond the purchase price to put it in first-rate shape?

The last fading smudge of sunset was fast disappearing. The lane seemed very dark. There was an almost eerie quality to the ragged trees arching overhead. Even when she had come with the full committee, in broad daylight, the place had seemed ghostly, although she would never have admitted it if the mice hadn't scuttled about in the wall and made them all jump. But what could one expect of an enormous house that had stood vacant for the past seven years? It's a wonder there was anything left of it at all!

She had stopped by the realty office earlier to pick up a key, but now it was getting so dark she was afraid to turn up the driveway. Heaven only knew what broken glass or jagged can was waiting there to puncture a tire. She really hadn't meant to come alone in the first place. She decided to stop in the lane, just to have another look. Well, there it was, of course, just as big, just as darkly handsome as ever. Silly, she told herself, it wasn't going to just disappear, not after it had been there for over fifty years. It had been built with all the extravagance of the 1920's and really never put to constant use after the Depression. There had been a succession of renters, the last

ones hippies who had been evicted. Now nothing remained of the original Hoppers except their name, a host
of garbled legends, and a snarled estate that was on the
verge of being settled.

"Well," she thought, "no matter. Mrs. Conway told
me I could keep the key until tomorrow, and I'll just ask
Edna and any of the other committee members who want
to, to come out with me."

"But isn't that strange?" she said aloud this time. "For
just the briefest moment I thought I saw a faint light on
in one of the basement windows. How very odd!"

It was odd, indeed. Mrs. Conway had said nothing
about another party's being interested in looking at the
house. Well, whatever it was, was gone. "Don't be ridiculous," Mrs. Murdoch said, driving on. "The power isn't
even connected! It was only a reflection."

3

"Mom——" Kerry slung her dirty warm-ups on top of the washing machine as she came in. "Are they going to do anything with the old Hopper House?"

"Why?" Sandra Blake was at the kitchen table, typing.

"I just wondered. It's a neat old place."

"Well," Sandra said and left it hanging in the air absentmindedly. She made a notation and slipped a clean piece of paper into the typewriter. "How'd practice go?" She sounded as she usually did when she was hard at work, as if she really didn't know what she was saying. It was almost automatic. Sometimes Kerry wished her mother didn't have to write articles; when she was working she couldn't think of anything else.

Kerry said, "Coach told me if I grew another inch I could jump center. Big deal! I'm already taller than most of the guys in my class. Anything to eat?"

"There's some soup in the refrigerator."

"Soup! Again?"

"It's almost gone. Beggars can't be choosers. Much homework?"

"I did most of it in study period." Kerry opened the refrigerator and looked inside to see if there was anything else besides soup. She was starved. "Did you eat the last piece of pie?"

"Pie?"

"Mom, don't you ever hear anything I say? I mean, really listen to me?"

Sandra sighed, leaned back in her chair, and stretched. "I'm sorry, honey. I really did hear you. It's just that I've got a deadline tomorrow, and that requires a lot of concentration. Yes, I ate the pie. That's all I had time for. I ate it for lunch. What about the old Hopper place?"

"I just wondered if anybody bought it."

Sandra got up and took the saucepan from Kerry, gave her a kiss on the cheek, and started heating the soup. "I haven't heard that it's actually been sold. But rumor's out that the local Gray Power fine arts committee is trying to get the city to put up funds for it."

"Gray Power?"

"Retirees. Senior citizens. The 'gray' comes from the color of their hair."

"Don't tell me a bunch of doddering old people are going to buy that wonderful place!"

"Don't knock it, honey. With people living longer and

the birth rate going down, Gray Power is going to be *the* power one of these days. And, unless you plan to jump off a bridge, you'll be one of them soon enough." She put the bowl of hot soup in front of Kerry, kissed the top of her ruffled hair, and sat opposite her. "Sorry it isn't a steak," she said, "but it's—"

"—full of meat and vegetables, and the vitamins are hopping all over the place," Kerry finished for her. "I know."

"Well, don't knock that either. It's been a long month so far, and we're broke, lamb pie."

"Mom, what if I got a job after school? I could drop basketball and—"

"Over my dead body."

"But then—"

"Kerry, we've been through all that. We have all the basics we need, soup into the bargain. We have a nice little apartment here, even though it is small, but the rent is about as low as we'll find. And we wouldn't be down to soup now, except I had to have a tooth filled, and that set us back. But you're not to worry. Your father left us with enough insurance to hold us, with my article sales helping out. It's just tough that what he thought was going to be an ample allowance for us has been eaten up by inflation. But that's the way it is. And there are many, many people in the same boat. Gray Power people most of all."

"I don't see what they would do with a big old house like that even if they *did* buy it."

"They're not dead, Kerry. They want a place for all

sorts of activities. They want the stimulation of learning new hobbies. Of writing and painting, putting on plays and music. You don't realize what a tremendous cross-section of talent is there. Retired teachers, retired musicians, and just plain Aunt Nellies who always wanted to do those things but never had time for it while they were working or raising a family. And they want the companionship an arts center would give them. I think it's a great idea."

Kerry finished the last drop of soup. "Hey, isn't there even a cookie?"

"How about an orange?"

Kerry watched her mother as she got the orange. She was a pretty woman, small, delicately boned, all the things that Kerry thought were desirable. All the things she would like to be, but knew she would never be, as she just grew and grew and left her little mother looking up at her, even when she was hopping mad and bawling Kerry out.

Suddenly Kerry blurted, "Mom, do you think you'll ever get married again?"

It had come out unexpectedly, and Kerry saw her mother wince, saw the instant look of pain, almost as if Kerry had struck her. Sandra stared down at the gold band on her finger, turning it, saying nothing.

The unwanted question had been growing in Kerry for a long time, like a noxious weed. It consumed her. She had adored her father, and the past five months had been hell. Just plain hell. She wondered if she would ever adjust to the feeling of total loss she felt at his sudden death. Their whole life had been turned upside down. Her mother had sold their house on the other side of town, the one Kerry had grown up in, and that meant leaving the only neighborhood she had ever known, leaving all of her friends.

Then her mother had found this small garage apartment, and that meant a new school for Kerry, a school she had always considered a rival. She'd heard about the wrong side of the tracks, and even though a railroad wasn't involved, this side of town was considered run-down and crummy. And she couldn't figure out why her mother had decided to move here, anyway. There were lots of small houses and apartments near their old neighborhood. It was as if her mother had deliberately got rid of every part of their old life, and it didn't make any sense.

Now Sandra answered, as if there hadn't been that long, agonized pause.

"I can't tell the future, Kerry. If I could, maybe I would have foreseen—maybe prevented—"

"Mom—don't. I'm sorry." Kerry felt ashamed, and the anguish deepened. "Nobody knows what's going to happen. You couldn't have done anything different. I shouldn't have asked you that, anyway."

Sandra lifted her head, her soft brown hair curling about a pretty face with wide green eyes. "And why shouldn't you ask?"

"It's none of my business."

"Listen, honey. If I am ever lucky enough to meet a man as—" She broke off, and Kerry saw her swallow hard. Then Sandra said, "If I should meet the right guy, you'll be the only one whose opinion I'll ask. You'll be the first to know."

Kerry nodded. A sudden wave of love, mixed with an unexpected, overwhelming sense of relief flowed from her to her mother.

"It's a good orange, Mom," she said, because that was all she trusted herself to say. Tears were always too close to the surface to try to say more.

4

Carl wondered how much longer they were going to wait. They had reached the big old vacant house in Blanton the night before, and, although Ax had told him nothing, Carl figured something must have gone wrong. They shouldn't be hanging around like this. The way he understood it from the little he did know, part of the plan was to drop the stuff and get out as quickly as possible. Then the pickup or transfer bunch, or whoever took over from there, would handle the rest of the job while he and Ax would be reassigned to new partners and another job. At least that was how it had been that first time when he and crazy Dinghy had left the silver and jewelry back in

Florida. Another old deserted place like this, only much smaller.

The big basement room where they had spent the night was clammy and sour with old trash. Things had run through the walls, the rafters all night. Carl was reminded of all he had read and seen on TV of old-time steamships—huge boiler rooms where sweating guys stoked huge furnaces like the one in the room where they had stowed their stash. The bowels of the ship, they had always been called. Now he knew why.

But now he wasn't sweating, except from his nerves: he was cold. Jesus, he'd never *been* so cold! Or hungry. They had finished the last of the sandwiches for breakfast. That was hours ago.

Ax was sitting with his back against the wall under a small overhead window, a gray, cruel-looking ghost of a man, smoking. He held a paper cup on one knee as an ashtray. The sandwich wrappings, the crumbs, had been carefully collected and wadded into the paper bag they'd brought them in. And there Ax sat like a lady at a damned tea party, carefully flicking the ashes from his cigarette into the paper cup when Carl *knew* they were supposed to be gone and *out* of there.

He could feel his nervousness and his aversion to the man rising dangerously. If Ax was going outside of orders, Carl thought he deserved to know.

"Why the wait?" he asked.

"A change of plan." The few times Ax had said anything, Carl had been surprised by the soft, slow voice.

"Whose plan?"

"You'll find out," Ax said softly.

"I'd like to know now."

The scar puckered into a smile. Ax tilted his head back against the wall, the cigarette hanging from the crooked smile. Little puffs of smoke came out as he chuckled to himself. "All in good time."

"Now," Carl demanded.

"We're waiting for Benny."

"Who the hell is Benny?"

Ax chuckled again. "Benny is an old, old acquaintance."

"What's that got to do with this? With the job? With us?"

"Us?" Ax said.

"Me!"

The man looked at Carl for several seconds. "Benny and I have a score to settle," he said. "An old, old score."

Carl hunched forward. "Look," he said. "What's between you and Benny, or anybody else, has nothing to do with me. I don't want any part of it."

Ax said nothing.

"We're supposed to be out of here," Carl went on. "We're supposed to be long gone. That was the order."

Still Ax said nothing. He sat quietly, staring almost dreamily at the rafters in the basement room. The light from the little window over his head groped duskily into the gloom of dampness, laying a pall of gray on the sharp profile. Carl felt his anger turning white hot inside him, the anger he had never learned to control, now all mixed up with the fear and frustration. He strained toward Ax, letting the bigness of his young male self loom over the little man.

"I'm getting out!" he said.

Ax blew more smoke.

Carl shouted again, "I'm getting out! You hear?"

Ax turned his head slowly. "Where to?"

"Just out. Away! You can't—"

He stopped. Suddenly the light from the little window grew dim. Ax's profile no longer chiseled the gloom. Carl blinked, then turned, looking overhead.

"Shut up," Ax said. He squashed out the butt of his cigarette against his shoe, dropped it carefully into the cup.

The two listened intently. Carl could hear the soft rustle of dead leaves outside the small window. Soft footsteps.

Ax leaned near Carl's ear. "If it isn't Benny, we're the power company to check the wires. You will keep your mouth shut. I know what I'm doing."

Sandra hurried up the steps, not waiting for the elevator, walked rapidly down the hall, and pushed through the doors of the newsroom of the Blanton *Morning Herald*. She put her neat brown envelope on the editor's desk and blew out a sigh.

Natalie Powers waved to her from across the space of desks and clacking typewriters.

"Sandy," she called. "Got a minute?"

Sandra liked Natalie. Natalie was one of the few women she knew who had been able to move up in a tough, male-dominated profession. Not only moved up successfully to associate editor, but never once lost sight of herself as a woman.

Now Sandra wove a broken-field pattern around to Natalie's desk. "That was close," she said, sinking into the vacant chair. "I didn't think I'd make that deadline."

Natalie looked at her watch and smiled. "Two minutes to spare. How altruistic are you feeling these days?"

"When I get paid for that job, I might forget my hunger pangs and feel very public-spirited. What favor are you about to ask me to do?"

"It's this senior citizens' group. They are after an art center for the city. A Mrs. Murdoch called me this morning to ask if we could help with publicity."

"I thought all groups had eager publicity chairmen and all we had to do was smooth out their copy."

"Well," Natalie said, "there will be some of that, too. But this might be a bit bigger than most projects. It seems, according to Mrs. Murdoch, that Allen Davidson —he's third-ward councilman—told her he would like to see the project get off the ground. He's not on the finance committee, but he feels she can get somewhere with the council as a whole if she'll broaden her approach."

"And?"

"And Davidson suggests maybe a series on it with a big wrap-up in a Sunday edition. With pictures."

"I don't even own a Brownie."

"Well, if there's anything in it we can use on that scale, we can give you a photographer."

"So what do you want me to do?"

Natalie picked up a pencil and rolled it between her palms thoughtfully. "I suppose the first thing would be to make a date with her—to fill you in on the whole bit. The history."

"What about Mr. Davidson? Does he want to get really involved?"

"It's an angle, certainly. And it would draw more attention if he were willing to stick his neck out for it."

"Have you talked to him yourself?"

"No. Not yet. But maybe he'd be willing to meet with you and Mrs. Murdoch just to let you know what would be the most attractive approach. Maybe he has some concrete ideas. She mentioned something about three articles with *punch*! That's the way she said it. You have any *punchy* ideas?"

Sandra laughed. "Not right off the bat, but maybe something will surface. We *are* talking about the old Hopper House, aren't we? Or was that just rumor?"

"No. That's it. Mrs. Murdoch seems to have researched it all very thoroughly. Why don't you get everything you can on it, and let's see how it breaks down into a series?"

"Freebies, huh?"

"I'm afraid so. But I'll throw you the next good-paying job we have." Natalie shot her a sideways glance. "And if I were you, I'd involve Allen Davidson whether he wants to get involved or not."

Sandra asked, "Am I reading wicked messages in those blue eyes?"

"Just dropping hints. He's a very nice man and probably the last of the gentlemen bachelors."

"I thought all bachelors past the age of thirty had something wrong with them."

"He's not one by choice."

"Meaning?"

"Meaning I don't think he's found the right person. I should know. I tried out for the part."

Sandra drew an uncertain breath. The banter was no good. The ache of loneliness she had lived with for the five months since Ted's death went too deep.

"Sandy," Natalie said gently, "come back to the world. It's the only way. I know what you're feeling—believe me. I've been there, only not for the same reasons, but a split is a split whether it's divorce or death."

"I—I don't think I'm ready."

"It can't be forced. I know that too. But it has to be given a chance. He's a very nice guy, Sandy."

Sandra bit her lip. Then she forced a smile. "I'll call you when I get a story worth looking at."

She stood up and started toward the door, holding the wavering smile until she got out into the hall. There she stopped at the drinking fountain and wet her dry lips.

Coach had let the team off practice early because of a teachers' meeting, and Kerry looked forward to the extra time it would give her to poke around the old Hopper place. Now that there was the possibility of its being sold, she felt a new urgency to go there and have it all to herself as long as she could.

She turned her bike into Hopper's Lane, pedaled around the curve, and braked to a stop. Somebody was sitting on her knoll.

"Jeff!" she called. "What in the world are you doing here this time of day?"

He threw a pebble at a spot in the road. "Waiting for you. I figured you'd get off early."

"Yes, but—you didn't run here. You've still got on your school clothes."

"Well, maybe I just needed to talk to somebody."

She pushed her bike to its resting place against the yellow poplar and sat down beside him. He threw another pebble.

Then Kerry asked, tentatively, "Are you okay?"

"Scared." Another pebble and she waited. "I have to go see the doctors this afternoon." He took a deep breath. "Kerry, I just don't know if I can take it if they say anything else about another operation!"

"But you've been doing great, Jeff! Why should they operate now?"

"The dumb bones—they aren't sure they're elongating or whatever bones are supposed to do."

She tried to think of something encouraging to say. "Do they know you can come this far? You don't even limp the way you used to. Do they know you can jog a little?"

"It was a test. 'Go ahead,' " he mimicked sarcastically. " 'See if it works.' But I don't think they—well, I just don't believe they thought it would work."

Kerry turned on him. "Well, just *tell* them it works!

For heaven's sake, Jeff, you'll be back on the track by spring at this rate."

"Yeah," he said without conviction.

"You *are* scared, aren't you? Don't be, Jeff. They do have to check, you know. It's just routine to check."

"Yeah—with the whole orthopedic clinic turning out to make the big decision." He stood up. "Well, I gotta go get showered. Prepare the bod and all that."

He offered a hand to pull her up. He wasn't very tall when she was standing next to him, but at least he was taller than she was. She liked his looks—the wide friendly smile and hazel eyes that slanted up at the corners as if he'd seen something funny. Only now he wasn't smiling.

He said, "I suppose you're going to go stare at your old house."

Kerry blushed, confused because he sounded cross.

"Well," he said, "I still don't think it's a good idea— hanging around an old abandoned place like this by yourself. You don't know who might be in there, some tramp or bunch of kids raising Cain."

"There's never been anyone around," she said. "Besides, it's probably locked."

"Look—I know I can't say anything to make you *not* want to go up there. But—Kerry, I wish you wouldn't."

"What's going to hurt if I just maybe peek in a window?"

He shrugged. "Well, just be careful, okay?"

She laughed. "Okay."

He turned away. "I gotta go."

"Jeff, call me. I want to know how you come out. Please?"

"Sure. I'll let you know. See you. And you watch out for the boogie-bears."

There was no humor in the way he said it, and he started walking away.

"Good luck!" Kerry called after him. He didn't turn, but waved back over his shoulder.

Suddenly she felt depressed. Jeff *was* worried. About himself, about her, too, and she hated that. She turned away from his dejected figure and sat down.

She looked up at her house. It really is *my* house, she thought. And today she had plenty of time to explore around.

Only now it wasn't the same. The old magic had gone out of it, and she concentrated hard to bring it back. She wished Jeff could have stayed, that he wasn't so worried about his leg, that—so many things.

She stood up. *"Now,"* she thought. And she started up the curving drive. It seemed much steeper than she had thought. And much longer. The house almost seemed to be retreating from her, sliding back farther up the hill.

She stopped a minute, not knowing just why she hesitated, but feeling an unwelcome strangeness, as if a cold wind had started up.

"It was that silly Jeff and his boogie-bears," she told herself.

But the house seemed very big and very lonely. The windows stared blankly at her from behind the shroud of ivy.

"There *can't* be anybody in there," she told herself. "That's just stupid. Of course it's empty! And this is just the chance I've been waiting for."

Then, squaring her shoulders, she walked on up toward the house.

5

Sandra had gone through her closet, and now she stared down at the three skirts laid across the bed, unable to decide what to wear. She had put in a call to Mrs. Murdoch and Mr. Davidson when she left Natalie and was surprised that they both readily agreed to meet with her at four o'clock. Mr. Davidson had suggested his office, and now that the time was nearing for her to dress and get over there, she felt absolutely drained.

If only she could go to this interview with nothing more on her mind than gathering facts. If only Natalie had not said anything about Allen Davidson. It was the hint of something more, of a face-to-face she was not ready for, that unsettled her. She was too aware of the trauma women faced in starting back into circulation after losing their husbands one way or the other, and all accounts had terrified her. She had never thought she would be one of them, but now she wondered for the first time if she shouldn't begin to meet men. For Kerry's sake, if not for her own. Kerry missed Ted more than she let on, Sandra knew, and certainly something precious had gone out of her life that somehow should be replaced. But how could you ever replace Ted?

Sitting on the edge of the bed, Sandra slowly twisted the ring from her finger. A definite indented mark circled the place where it had been for twenty years. Her finger looked very naked, and as she stared at it an invisible vise tightened around her chest.

She remembered the wedding rehearsal, when Ted had pretended to be so nervous that he stuck the ring on her thumb instead of her finger. The hilarious hubbub of trying to get it off, with the whole rehearsal party pulling on it, had made her thumb swell. Her mother finally called the hospital for advice. The solution was simple enough: wrap thread tightly all the way from the ring to the tip of the thumb, soap heavily, and work the ring off.

How sheepish Ted had looked! Then they started to laugh, falling into each other's arms, laughing until they were breathless. Oh, God, she thought, how many crazy times like that there had been—laughter, fun, and, yes, some knocks too. But always the scales had swung back to a lovely balance.

Now, with a feeling of physical sickness, she crossed to her dressing table, opened her jewelry box, and gently placed the ring inside. She dressed, left a note for Kerry saying where she would be and that she might be late getting home, then went down the steps of the little garage apartment to her car.

All the way to town she thought of nothing but the last few days of Ted's illness. He had been struck down so suddenly that there was no time for them to communicate, to say those things that need to be said when one partner is going to leave the other. They had shared a unique closeness, and now she was consumed with an unreasonable, yet very real, feeling that what she was doing was wrong. She wished she had never taken that lovely, simple, enduring symbol from her finger. She pulled into the parking space in front of the insurance offices and turned off the ignition. With her hands still on the steering wheel she rested her head against them a moment.

"This is ridiculous," she thought. "I'm not a kid, and I do need to try. Natalie was right, of course. I should at least try."

But she could not shake the unwillingness: it was there, and it would not go away.

It had all happened so fast, Carl didn't have time to think. He and Ax had heard the steps outside in the dead leaves, the sliding sound of something opening, either a window or a door, the echoing footsteps in the huge empty hall overhead. Then Ax motioned Carl beneath the stairwell while he positioned himself behind a cement column.

Carl heard the cellar door squeal open, the heavy footsteps descending. Then Ax's soft, icy voice.

"Hello, Benny."

From his hiding place Carl heard the sharp intake of breath. The other man said, "I suppose this is a coincidence."

The low chuckle. "Isn't it strange, Benny? Us here together? Does it strike you as odd after all these years?"

There was a pause. Then, "What do you want, Ax?"

"Several things, Benny. First, I want to know what you came to pick up here."

"I'm not going to pick up anything."

"Oh, Benny! Come on! I know it for a fact, and besides we've both been in this business too long for that. What other reason would you be here?"

"What do you want?" he repeated. His voice was thick.

"Come on out, Carl," Ax said.

Carl ducked out from under the stairs.

"This is Carl, Benny."

The fat man looked at him, then back at Ax. He shrugged his round shoulders. "All right, so there are two of you."

"Cut us in, Benny," Ax said.

"No."

"As big a take as that, huh? Look, Carl likes to scare people. Look how big he is, Benny. Much bigger than you are. Just because he's a kid doesn't mean he can't break you in half."

Carl didn't know what kind of a game Ax was playing. He felt he was being sucked into something he had not bargained for, but he didn't know just what to do about it. All he could really do was wait and see what developed. Maybe there would be something in it for him. Just be cool and think, he told himself. And watch. You don't know which side you're on yet. But he didn't like it at all. He wanted to be long gone from there and from them both.

Ax said, "I found out there's a double dip here, Benny. What we brought and what you're supposed to pick up. And I didn't hear your car."

"I didn't bring one."

The snarled eyebrows lifted. "A clue? Something you can carry away without a car?"

Benny's round face relaxed into a damp smile. "We've both got an advantage, Ax. You with him, and me with what I know. Shall we bargain?"

Though the smile remained on Benny's fat face, Carl read danger in his eyes. As Benny's left hand inched slowly to his coat pocket, Carl lunged at him, pinning him against the column, wrenching his left arm up and behind his back. With a metallic clank a .38 revolver hit the basement floor. Instantly Ax leaned over and picked it up. Then he ran his hands over Benny, searching him.

Carl said, "What should I do with him?"

"Hold him. I'm going out to the van and get something to tie him up with. Then we'll just sit here and wait. I think he'll want to share the secret."

Getting into the old mansion was not as hard as Kerry had thought it might be. She had circled around the huge main part. No windows open there. Front door bolted.

Now she peered through one of the long windows of the left wing. She cupped her hands around her eyes, her face close to the smudged glass.

The large room she saw was empty; several doors opened from it to other parts of the house. As she cocked her head to try for a look down the long hallway beyond, she leaned against the window and the glass moved slightly. She stepped back, surprised. Then she placed her hands flat against the pane and pressed upward. Slowly the window slid partway open. Excited now, she raised it enough to crawl through, then looked around for something high enough to stand on so she could climb in.

She found a squarish rock, shoved it underneath the window, got up on it, and pulled herself to the window ledge. "My gosh!" she thought. "I'm in!" and she lowered her feet to the floor of the big room inside.

The air in the house was cold and dead, like a tomb. She listened a minute, but the only sound was her quick breathing. Then slowly she tiptoed toward the door she felt would lead to the main section in front. She wanted to see what kind of parlor this big old house had, maybe a ballroom even, see if it was as wonderful as she had dreamed.

When she reached the hallway she stopped. "Why am I tiptoeing?" she asked herself. And with that she walked as casually and deliberately as she could make herself, into the high-ceilinged room that served as the front entrance hall.

Ornate paneling ran from ceiling to floor, dull with years of dust. She crossed to another door, pushed it open, and found herself at last in a drawing room of such proportions that she felt dwarfed. The domed ceiling was full of fancy curlicues and figures, and she looked at the place where a chandelier should have been. Only an ugly broken place in the stained ornamental ceiling remained; a piece of heavy black-covered wire, frayed and grotesque, hung from the hole. The air in here seemed deader and colder than ever and she moved instinctively to the enormous fireplace.

How beautiful it must have been, she thought, to sit before a fire here and watch it flicker on the wide mahogany mantelpiece. She turned full-faced toward the fireplace, visualizing handsome brass andirons with huge logs blazing on them, and she held her hands out to the imagined warmth. There would be big wing chairs drawn before it, a table between them for wineglasses on a silver tray, and she would sit with her feet propped carelessly on a velvet footstool and sip Madeira.

Or maybe she'd have an orchestra in and have a dance. She would throw a huge ball and dance all night. Imagining herself dressed in a dazzling gown, she lifted her arms to embrace an invisible partner and whirled about in the first step of a waltz.

As she turned, her song choked to a terrified stop in her throat. There stood the ugliest little man she had ever seen. He was pointing a gun at her.

"Don't move," he said. "And don't make a sound. Leave your hands up."

Her whole body went rigid as he searched her, touching her all over, the sickening odor of stale cigarettes and coffee hot in her face. Her stomach heaved with fear and the utter shock of what was happening to her.

"All right," he said. "Walk in front of me." And he jammed the point of the pistol in her back.

Carl had begun to get nervous. Ax was taking forever to bring back the damned rope. How much longer could he hold Benny with his head shoved down, his left arm twisted up behind him? Jesus, what a mess. That goddam Ax was screwing the whole deal. Carl had half a mind to let Benny loose and just get the hell out of there. But he heard footsteps overhead and knew Ax was coming back. He'd have to wait now. For what, he didn't know. Just wait.

The basement door opened above, and Carl looked up. A girl stood there, frozen, like a startled animal. Carl turned cold. What now? Then he heard Ax say, "Start walking down."

When they reached the foot of the stairs, Ax gave her a shove forward.

"She belong to you, Benny?" he demanded.

Benny raised his head as far as he could before Carl pushed it down again. "I never saw her in my life."

"Why don't you tell her we're the goddam power company!" Carl exploded.

"Shut up, Carl." Ax motioned in front of him with the nose of the gun. "You, girl, you and Benny sit down. Right there, Benny. Then when you're ready, tell me what you came for."

"Please," the girl begged, "please—let me go! I—"

Ax swung the muzzle toward her. "Sit down," he said in his quiet voice.

Carl watched the girl's face. She was scared silly, he knew that, but she didn't sit down.

"They're right behind me," she said. She licked her lips. "There are two carloads of them, maybe more. It's —it's my whole basketball team. They all want to see this house. Let me go, and I'll tell them it's locked up and we can't get in."

Ax held her with a hard stare. She didn't flick an eyelash. If she was lying, Carl sure couldn't tell, and he figured neither could Ax.

"Get up," Ax said to Benny. "Keep his arm behind him, Carl. You, girl. You walk in front of me."

"Where are you taking her?" Carl demanded. He didn't want any more complications than he already had.

"We're all going to get in the van," Ax said. "We'll park it down below and wait. If this kid isn't lying, we'll know soon enough. If she is, Benny will have plenty of time to tell us what he came for."

Still holding the .38 in front of him, Ax scooped up the butt-filled paper cup and the bag of trash.

"Move," he said in his soft voice and motioned them up the stairs with the point of Benny's gun.

6

Allen Davidson had been talking to the two women in his small office for some time when he suddenly realized he had been unconsciously comparing them. Like Mrs. Murdoch, Sandra Blake dressed simply. Her light-beige skirt was a becoming length that did the most for a pair of very nice legs. The beige of the skirt was repeated in a soft wool cardigan that topped an equally soft blouse. He particularly liked the way the green figure in the scarf matched the dark-fringed green eyes. Sandra Blake carried her fortyish years as well as Mrs. Murdoch carried her seventy-odd. But there the similarity ended.

While Mrs. Murdoch appeared flushed with excitement at the potential this meeting held for advancing her cause, Sandra Blake seemed withdrawn. She was efficient, to be sure, cassette recorder for taking notes, pad and pencil ready. And she had carried off the interview admirably so far with a good list of guiding questions.

But where was the enthusiasm? Did she lack enthusiasm just for this particular job, he wondered, or was something missing in Sandra Blake herself? Not for a long time had he encountered such an attractive woman with so—well, so closed a look. Or was he misreading a natural reserve, a pronounced sense of privacy? It was puzzling. Still, an aura of mystery always aroused his interest.

Then he realized she was saying something and he was not listening.

"Natalie Powers," she repeated, "mentioned a broader approach. Do you have something definite in mind?"

He coughed to give his mind time to catch up, and leaned forward. "Yes. I was very interested in Mrs. Murdoch's presentation to the council. I talked informally to some of the members later and I think they feel such a center should serve the whole community. The young as well as senior citizens. That is my position, too, and I think that's the only way the idea will appeal to the finance committee. Certainly from what I gathered it would have a better chance with the council as a whole."

The sparkle of confidence went out of Mrs. Murdoch's eyes and she blinked. "That simply would not do," she said.

"Why not?"

"Oh, good heavens!" She laughed lightly. "Because we had in mind a quiet place. A sort of retreat. Young people play that awful, loud electronic music. And they tend to be very messy and inconsiderate. No. That isn't what we had in mind at all."

"It's a big house," Sandra said. "It has two big wings." She pointed to the architect's sketches Mrs. Murdoch had spread on the desk earlier. "Perhaps something could be worked out, using this central area as a buffer zone."

Allen said, "For one thing we could involve other areas of community services such as parks and recreation. And we could get the kids who would use the facilities involved in the actual renovation. Not only the kids, but everybody. It could be a big cohesive project for the whole town. Work parties, suppers on the grounds—that sort of thing. We could involve churches and civic groups. I think it would sell itself that way."

Sandra's pencil was making quick notes again.

"And," he went on, "it would make a beautiful series of articles. Follow it all the way—you know the sort of thing. Before-and-after shots. Nice human-interest touches." He was getting more excited about it by the moment himself. "And don't forget, even if we get the initial capital for the center, it will have to be maintained. We could harness some of those kids' energy for that too. That way they would feel a share of the responsibility for it. I think they would take pride in it—don't you agree?"

"Well," Mrs. Murdoch said reluctantly, "perhaps that would be true. But that isn't what we want."

"Look," Allen said. "I haven't actually been inside the

house, although I've driven by several times. Would you ladies be free right now to run over there with me? Maybe an on-site tour would give us a better idea of what we're talking about. Mrs. Murdoch?"

"Yes, I'm free. And I still have the key I picked up yesterday."

He looked at Sandra.

"My daughter will be getting home from basketball practice in a little while," she said. "But I don't live far from there. I can take my own car."

He didn't know why this disappointed him. Perhaps he had thought they might get better acquainted on the drive. It was while she was gathering up her note pad and recorder that he noticed her hands. Pretty, capable hands that looked as if they could also be very gentle. As he was appraising them she stopped in the midst of what she was doing, and he saw the hands grow tense. It was then that he saw her ring finger, saw the telltale impression of a band removed not long ago.

"Well," he said to himself, "Allen, you romantic fool. Mystery, my foot! She's just another newly divorced woman who's not over the hump of separation and has a sizable grudge on for the world. There's your 'vague mysterious withdrawal,' you idiot!"

But when he raised his eyes to hers, the stricken, somehow guilty look of panic swimming in their green depths took him completely by surprise. He wanted very much to say something, although he didn't for the life of him know what he could say under the circumstances. But the moment passed. She slung the strap of her purse abruptly over her shoulder, muttered something about meeting them at the Hopper House, and hurried out of his office.

The back of the van was dim. Ax had shoved Kerry roughly inside and told her to lie on the floor. She lay curled up, nearly covered by the canvas they had thrown on top of her. She was next to the fat man, Benny, and she didn't want to touch him. He smelled bad.

The man called Ax had double-locked the back of the van, then got in the front seat with the other one—the boy called Carl. Although they sat with their backs to her and Benny, she knew they were watching them in the rearview mirror.

The sound of her heart pounded in her ears. Her only hope was that they wouldn't notice her bike leaning against the yellow poplar. If anything should happen to her, the bike was the only thing that might tell someone where she had been. That and Jeff Andrews. He knew she had been on this dirt road; he had seen her, and he knew she was going up to the house. If something did happen to her, Jeff would recognize the bike. He was going to call her about the doctors' report on his leg, and when he found out she was missing, they'd look here. They'd find the bike. They'd know. But know what? What did they plan to do with her? How long would they stay parked here?

She wanted to pray but was afraid the intensity of her prayers might stir up some ESP waves. She was terrified to even think about the bike.

Oh, dear God. Surely nothing will happen to me! Surely they'll unlock the back of the van and let me go.

What are they doing here anyway? What secret does Benny have that they want to know? And why were they in the house in the first place? There had never been anybody on this road before except Jeff. But they had hidden the van behind the summerhouse, so maybe they had been there before and she had not noticed.

Her mind raced with half-formed ideas of escape. She tried desperately to think of something else to say that would scare them into letting her go. If only another car *would* come along, maybe they would believe it was the basketball team. Maybe they would let her out then, make her promise not to say anything. Maybe they would leave then and not come back. Ever!

She could hear the scared breathing of the fat Benny whistling in his throat. And she could hear a watch ticking; it was her own. It was five thirty. She should be going home. Oh, if only she were there now, how wonderful that little garage apartment would look! How long would her mother wait before she began to worry? Would she call the school?

Then Ax said, "Is that your bike, kid?" and her heart sank.

She swallowed. "I don't have a bike."

"Well, how did you get here?"

"I—my boyfriend brought me. Jeff Andrews dropped me off, and he's coming back for me."

"Whose bike is that?"

No one said anything, and Ax turned, looking down at her with that scar dragging the edge of his eye. "Whose bike?" he asked again softly.

She shook her head. "I don't know."

He turned back to Carl. "What do you think?"

Carl blurted, "How the hell should I know?"

Ax looked back at her again. "Hey, kid," he said in that awful soft voice, "you wouldn't be lying?"

"Why should I lie?" Her voice began to waver, and she wished he would turn away so she wouldn't have to look at him. It would be so much easier.

"Carl," he said then, "get the bike."

"Why? Hell, suppose she's telling the truth? We take the bike, and it's not hers, all we do is alert somebody that something is wrong. Let's just dump them and get out of here!"

"She's lying," Ax said. "She's lying about the bike and about the boyfriend and about the basketball team. Get the bike."

Carl got out of the van. In a minute she could hear him unlocking the back. Then she felt a sharp pain in her shin as he threw the bike on top of her and Benny. She could see Carl for a moment framed in the square of light, huge and blond. He slammed the back shut, double-locked it, and got in front again.

"Ax, you better know what you're doing," he said.

"I know exactly what I'm doing."

"Well, how long we going to sit here? Why not just put them out and let's *go*, man!"

"Shut up."

"Well, then I'm getting out!"

"Wait," Ax said. "Because there *is* a car coming."

Kerry's heart leapt with new hope. She pulled her feet up, rolling slowly over to get them under her. Then she sprang up and forward toward the window and started screaming.

Ax wheeled in his seat and knocked her down, hard. She had caught only a glimpse of the road and had seen a car. But was it too far away to have heard her?

Ax said, "Don't pull any more tricks, do you understand?" The deadly calm of his soft voice was more terrible than if he had shouted.

A new panic began in the pit of her stomach: Ax had started the engine: the van began to move slowly.

Ax said, "Which tag did you put on, Carl?"

"Tennessee. Like you told me."

"Good." The van inched along, jolting over the ruts. As it turned out of the lane and onto Johnson Drive, Ax said, "That wasn't a basketball team, kid. It was only two people."

Carl looked behind in the side mirror. "Yeah," he said. "But there goes somebody else turning in there."

"Well, that does it." Ax's voice was softer, more ominous than ever. "We're heading out. Benny, you should have shared your secret when you had the chance."

Benny's breathing quickened; the whistling sound rose higher. "What are you going to do, Ax?"

"Let you sweat a little."

In desperation Kerry said, "My boyfriend knows where I am! He knows I was going to that house!"

"Sure, and maybe that's your basketball coach now and those other two were referees. You were in the wrong place at the wrong time, and now you're going for a long ride with us. You and Benny."

"If you put me out here, I couldn't get to a phone until you were gone. Nobody would know where to find you! I wouldn't say anything to anybody!"

"No. Of course you wouldn't."

"Please!" she cried. "Please let me go!"

"Don't make me have to hit you again, kid. Just shut up. As soon as we clear this town, Carl, tie them up and gag them."

The van moved faster now. She tried to concentrate, to keep the direction it was taking fixed in her mind. They had turned toward the freeway from Johnson Drive, and now they were heading west.

Then she said, "They'll know you left something in that house!"

Ax said, "Tell her, Carl."

Carl turned. "I don't know about what Benny was after, but there is no way anybody could find what we left without a blueprint."

"Now, shut up," Ax said. "Cover them good with the tarp, Carl. I don't want them or the bike to show."

Kerry felt the smart of tears begin, scratching the back of her throat and stinging her eyes. She held her fist tight against her mouth. "No," she thought, "don't cry. You can't cry. Think! Think of some way to get out of here!"

The air under the canvas was stale and moist with their breathing as she lay beside the fat, sweating Benny. She was aware of the sickening smell of gas sloshing in the cans beside her. Unable to see now, she lost all sense of direction. The van was not speeding, but it was going fast, and from the steadiness of its course she knew they must be on the freeway. But which way were they going? Nobody would notice a dark green van with a Tennessee license tag. Nobody would know she was inside under the acrid layer of canvas.

Suddenly she was filled with a hatred she had never known before in her life. She hated these three people. The feeling made her almost sick. She felt dirtied by it and unreal. It was worse than being afraid.

"Oh, God," she prayed, "please help me."

7

It was almost dark when Sandra let herself into the apartment. There were no lights on inside; Kerry was later than usual getting home. Sandra turned on the table lamp beside the couch, put the recorder and note pad on the kitchen table, then went to her tiny bedroom. There she put her ring back on her finger and closed the jewelry box. End of a foolish and unnecessary experiment. She richly deserved the results. In a housecoat and slippers she went back to the little kitchen and put on the kettle for a cup of tea.

She was tired. The whole afternoon had left her upset, emotionally drained. The tour of the Hopper House had not convinced Mrs. Murdoch that she and her fellow senior citizens could coexist with young people, and Sandra had left her and Mr. Davidson at a polite standoff as she hurried away.

Though she had used Kerry as an excuse to leave, she was almost glad Kerry wasn't home yet. It gave her a moment to sort out her thoughts, to try and shake the feeling that had come over her when Mr. Davidson had stared at her hands with such a knowing look. He had called her "Ms." the rest of the afternoon and only compounded her feeling of dislocation. She knew she had shut up more than her ring in the jewelry box. Beside it lay a large piece of her identity, and she was lost and miserable without it. When she left them, Mr. Davidson had said, "Thank you for your time, Ms. Blake," and she had said, "Please, it's Mrs. Blake," and his obvious embarrassment had only upset her more.

Now it didn't matter one way or the other about Mr. Davidson. She didn't even want to think about him. The kettle whistled. She made a cup of strong tea and took it to the couch, where she curled up against the cushions to wait for Kerry.

Finding she could not help thinking about Mr. Davidson, she switched on the TV. The news seemed even more repetitious and banal than usual, and she couldn't concentrate. After watching for a few minutes, she switched it off; then she checked the stove clock to see if her watch was right. It was completely dark outside.

"But Kerry's bike is equipped for night riding," she told herself. "So don't worry."

All the same, she did worry. Kerry was over an hour late. She had always been reliable about calling home if she was going to be delayed this long.

Sandra made another cup of tea, casting about for a reasonable explanation. She knew the school office would be closed, so there was no point in calling there. She was always reluctant to bother Kerry's teachers or her coach at home. Still, this was an unusual situation and a prickling apprehension grew by the minute.

She dialed the coach's number.

He was cordial as usual, Kerry being one of his favorites. But there had only been a short practice session that afternoon because of a teachers' meeting. No, he didn't know of any other school activity that could have detained her. In fact, because of the meeting everything else had been canceled or postponed.

Replacing the phone, Sandra stared blankly at the note pad beside it. Only the note she had left for Kerry stared back at her. Kerry had not been home. She would not have gone out again without leaving a message.

The tea had grown cold, and now Sandra poured it out and set the cup on the side of the sink. She looked out the kitchen window at the driveway below. She had not seen Kerry's bike when she came in, and she did not see it now. It and Kerry were still out somewhere. But why? And where?

Kerry had made a few friends since they had moved to this side of town and a check with them soon added to Sandra's concern: none of them had seen her after practice. They had no idea where she might be. When Sandra

called the last number, Jeff's, and there was no answer,
she sat on the edge of the couch, wondering what to do.
If Kerry were with Jeff, she would have called. Or Jeff
would have called. He was a good, responsible kid, and
he respected Sandra's rules when it came to Kerry. He
would have seen to it that Sandra received some sort of
message.

"The hospitals," she thought. "If there has been an
accident, Kerry might have been taken to one of the hospitals."

Back at the phone again, she made enquiries. Nothing.
She didn't know whether to be relieved or not. Maybe
something had happened and Kerry was lying beside the
road, injured, with no way to get help.

Quickly Sandra tore the top sheet from the note pad,
penciled another message saying she would be back in a
few minutes, changed to slacks and a sweater, then hurried down to the car.

Driving slowly, she retraced Kerry's route to school.
She knew about the shortcut Kerry had discovered, and
after going the old long way first, she doubled back,
turning this time up Hopper's Lane.

"Surely," Sandra thought, "if Kerry had been on this
road this afternoon, I would have seen her." Even as
miserably preoccupied with her uncomfortable situation as she had been, she would have noticed her own
daughter. But now there was no sign of Kerry or a bicycle anywhere.

When she came to the spot below the Hopper House,
Sandra stopped. Something in the back of her mind hov-

ered like a moth trying to get past a screen. Something about the house that afternoon had made a very dim impression on her numbness, and now she struggled to bring it to light.

She and Mrs. Murdoch and Allen Davidson had gone in the front door, Mrs. Murdoch furnishing the key. But what had Mrs. Murdoch said later? Where had they been in the house when Mrs. Murdoch had said—what?

They had gone first to the huge drawing room in the right wing. Then to illustrate the possible division of the house, they had returned to the central entrance hall, and then gone to the left wing. Yes. Now she remembered. It was while they were in the largest of the rooms there that Mrs. Murdoch had said, "Well! I see we wouldn't have needed a key. Look. There's a window open. Anyone could have got in."

But if Kerry had been in that house, why hadn't they seen her? Of course, they had only gone over the upper floors because of the growing darkness and Mrs. Murdoch's reluctance to chance the stairs to the basement level with no light. But surely there would have been a sign, some indication that Kerry was there, or had been there.

Slowly Sandra eased the car along the rest of the lane, up the steep hill, and onto Dexter Street. At the service station she stopped.

"Excuse me," she said to the attendant, who was busy with another car. "Did a girl on a bicycle stop here this afternoon for anything? Air in a tire—or something like that?"

"If she did, lady, I didn't see her. I just come on my shift at five."

"Well, is there anyone here who was on duty this afternoon?"

No, but he could give her a name and number to call. She thanked him and went to the pay phone. The man who answered her ring didn't remember seeing anyone, although he recognized the description of Kerry because she had stopped there before for a Coke. When? Oh, several days ago, he couldn't remember exactly. But he was sure he hadn't seen her that afternoon.

A call back to their apartment was not answered. Sandra let the phone ring a full three minutes. Even if Kerry had been in the shower, that would have given her time to answer. She was not there.

Now there was nothing to do but head slowly for home, looking for —what? And then, once again she was in the driveway of the apartment and her car lights struck blankly at the place Kerry's bike should have been.

A cold knot of panic lay in the pit of Sandra's stomach. Kerry loved the Hopper House. If that open window had been used by Kerry to get inside, couldn't someone else have gone in there the same way?

Terrified, Sandra left the car and ran up the steps to call the police.

At six o'clock Ax had stopped the van in a rest area and told Carl to tie and gag Kerry and Benny, then empty one of the cans of gas into the tank. Carl had put the bike outside while carrying out the order.

Then he asked, "Why don't we ditch the bike here?"

"No. They'll trace it. Otherwise nobody can connect a thing to us. Put it back inside."

Now Kerry figured three hours must have passed since Carl had tied them up. The van had been moving steadily along and she had no idea if they were north, east, south, or west of Blanton, or even if they were still in Georgia. She tried to visualize what her mother would be doing now. Would she have called the police?

Panic had given way to a sort of acceptance of her situation. There was nothing she could do now but think ahead. Although she did not feel exactly calm, she was clearheaded. And she was determined to keep alert for any opportunity to free herself. Meantime she would play a waiting game. This, she knew, would mean cooperating with Ax and Carl, lulling them into thinking she was no longer dangerous to them. Maybe they would even believe they could turn her loose, although she would not count on it. If you didn't count on things, then you didn't get let down. You could not be optimistic. Just realistic. And this she would try to be.

"There's a truck stop ahead," Carl said. "Do we eat? I've got to have something, man."

"We eat." Ax turned the van up the ramp, and then it stopped. "I'll see if I can get some gas. Are they covered good?"

"Buried."

"All right. You get us a couple of burger plates. I'll take care of the van."

"It'll look funny, you sitting out here."

"I won't be sitting. But I won't be two feet away, either."

"What about them?"

"Get two double orders. We don't want them to get sick on us. And fill the Thermos with coffee. We'll drive until I think it's safe to stop somewhere."

Under the canvas Kerry's mind began to whirl. She didn't know how far the diner was from the van or how long it would take Carl to get the food. But she would be able to tell when Ax got out. All right, think, she told herself. There should be something you can do while they're outside.

Benny shifted his position suddenly, and the pedal of the bike tore into Kerry's shin. She could tell the skin was broken from the sharp stinging. The bike must have settled hard on Benny, too, because he groaned. With her hands tied behind her back there was no way she could lift it off, so she tried to move out from under, to get the pedal out of her flesh. She brought her knees up as far as she could and with her bound feet pressed against the side of the van she pushed to a new position. And it was then that the bike's headlight bumped under her chin.

Now her brain began to work in earnest. She could hear people talking outside the van. If she could just get enough canvas off the bike, she could flash an SOS with the head lamp. No. Ax would see it. But even if he did, wouldn't somebody else see it, too, and help her? She wiggled around, but there was no way she could get the canvas off of her or the bike. She could feel herself begin to sweat.

"All right," she told herself, "so don't let it get you down. It's a good idea, and even if it won't work now, maybe it will later. You have to be patient. A time will come. It has to come, because they'll get tired. And then they'll get careless. Now stop thinking about the headlight or you'll stir up waves. What you *can* concentrate on and hope *does* stir up waves is a rest room. Surely they'll let you out for that soon. If Ax really doesn't want you to get sick, maybe he won't want your bladder to rupture, either. Concentrate. Then you could leave a message with soap on the mirror in the john. You could lock yourself in and there wouldn't be any way they could get you out. You could holler and people would come."

She could hear Ax outside. Was there an attendant there, too, or was Ax pumping the gas himself? She listened, but could hear no voices now. She knew the van wouldn't look strange at a truck stop, but what about Ax's face? Surely anyone who saw that ugly scar would remember him. If only she could think of some way to leave a clue that she, too, had been here!

Carl came back and she could smell the food even before he got in, but she had no appetite. The smell mingled with gas fumes and the musty air under the canvas. It was sickening.

"Now what?" Carl asked.

"We'll eat later," Ax said. "Stay here while I pay up. See if you can get a news report."

Carl turned on the radio. A syrupy string orchestra was playing "And I Love Her." The dial was switched, squawking, until Carl got a news station. Kerry hoped there would be a station break for identification, but the report was already in progress. There was nothing on it about a missing girl or a robbery or anything that would have any connection with Carl or Ax or Benny. At least if Benny had done any of the piddling things the reporter was talking about, she didn't see why Ax would have been so interested. No. What Ax and Carl and Benny had done was something pretty big.

Ax came back and Kerry heard the van creak as he got in. The door slammed, the engine started, and they moved away. Soon they were going steadily along what she was sure was a freeway, but the entrance to it had circled around so much that again she had no sense of direction or idea where they were. She'd never thought she'd yearn to see a billboard.

"Any report?" Ax asked.

"No."

"Pour me some coffee. Hold the plates until we get out of here. The Styrofoam should keep it hot."

Carl had turned the radio off, and now there was no sound except that of the van. There weren't even very many cars going along this highway.

At last they turned off again, and she assumed they would stop at another rest area. But the van began bumping over some rough pavement. She heard the sound of the tires change and smelled dust and knew they must be on a dirt road. After about two miles of this the van stopped.

"Okay," Ax said. "Untie them. We eat here."

The back of the van was unlocked, and Carl dragged

the canvas and bike off. The night air was cold after the stuffiness of being buried. Kerry could see stars through the back opening of the van until Carl got in and blotted out her view. His hands smelled of coffee as he untied and ungagged her.

"All right," Ax said, "get out."

Kerry felt stiff and numb as she climbed out. She drew a deep breath of fresh air and rubbed her wrists and ankles.

Then she said, "Please. I have to go to the bathroom."

"What do we do?" Carl asked.

"Take her behind that bush," Ax said.

"What about me?" Benny said.

"In front of the van."

Kerry had no idea where they were, except that the road looked like back country. There wasn't a house in sight. The beauty of the night surprised her. She had thought herself beyond appreciating anything except escape. Just to be untied had a certain wonderful quality about it, to stretch, to move, to be out of the van. And then to be relieved.

When she came from behind the bush, Carl grabbed her arm, although there was no need to. She would have gone back without prompting; there was no hope of escape in this strange place.

They sat on the ground under the stars. Suddenly the whole thing seemed out of kilter to Kerry. There she sat with three criminals, accepting a hamburger, drinking coffee as if they were on a picnic.

"These desperate people," she thought, "all with a

secret, and here I sit. It doesn't seem real. Carl is re-
filling my cup, and I should be hating them, but at this
minute I don't feel hate. It's like some sort of truce, or a
time-out in a rough basketball game. I don't feel anything except a strange floatiness. When I get back in that
van, when they tie me up again, I'll begin to feel the hate
again. But now I look at them and they look like ordinary people sitting here with me under these stars.
Maybe there is something basic in them, and in me, too,
something just human that can climb above being afraid.
But it seems weird that I should be thinking this now and
looking at that awful scar on Ax's face. Maybe Ax is like
he is because of that awful scar. But what about Carl?
And Benny?"

Then the spell was broken and she saw them as three
criminals again, and she was a captive, and she did not
sense anything human about them at all. It was time to
get back in the van.

"After you tie them up," Ax said, "put the Wisconsin
tag on."

"So even if someone at the truck stop did notice,"
Kerry thought, "it probably wouldn't do any good.
They'd get the description of the van wrong."

And then she lay once more, tied and gagged, and the
van was moving on—moving somewhere she knew
would make it harder and harder for anyone to find them.

8

Jeff Andrews tuned the radio to his favorite station. It was the only morning program that covered local events and sports. He had his bad leg propped on the desk in his room, and he tipped the chair back, listening.

Suddenly the program was interrupted.

". . . missing since yesterday afternoon. Anyone who has any information . . ."

His chair scraped the floor as he sat bolt upright. Something shot through him like a cold blade. No! Who? What? He leaned forward and turned the volume up so high that the repeated message blasted his ears.

My God! Kerry! But I just saw her yesterday—she can't be missing!

And then he remembered. He had tried to call her before his folks decided it would be nice to celebrate the good news about his leg and take the family out for dinner. There hadn't been any answer then, nor later, after they got back.

He turned the volume up even more, but the sportscaster had come on again. He looked at his watch. How could he possibly go to school today? Kerry had not been seen since yesterday afternoon. "Anyone who has any information . . ." The words echoed all through him.

And he slammed out of his room to the telephone.

". . . and so you see," Mrs. Murdoch said, "I don't think we should even try to set up another meeting. I do hate to be the bearer of bad news, but I felt I should tell you. Oh, that poor young woman! Her daughter missing!"

Allen Davidson was stunned. He thanked Mrs. Murdoch for her call, agreed that a meeting was out of the question, and slowly hung up the telephone. His hand remained on the receiver.

He had a vivid picture of Sandra Blake's eyes as he'd seen them the day before, the pain swimming in them, a private pain he knew nothing about. And now this. He barely knew Sandra Blake. What could he as a stranger do? He felt a reluctance to intrude; still he wanted very much to do something. Anything.

He called Tony Perez, chief of police.

"Not a thing, Allen. I've been trying to get you. We haven't much to go on except a kid reports he saw her yesterday afternoon about three thirty out Hopper's Lane way. On her bicycle. The day before he says he saw a dark green van with a Minnesota tag on the same road. Two males in it, but it was pretty dark so he couldn't give us a description. He didn't know the van make, either, and without the actual tag number, I don't think we'll get far. We were able to rush through the 'secure' procedure and get the magistrate's warrant for probable cause to search, so we're cleared to begin.

"Oh, and the kid told us about another car the same day he saw the van, but that's been explained. In fact, it was Mrs. Murdoch, who was out there with you and Mrs. Blake yesterday. She called today to report that the day before, when she had driven by the house, she thought she saw some kind of light in a basement window. She couldn't be sure and there's no power on out there now, so I don't know."

"Any way to connect the van to this?"

"We found tire tracks behind the summerhouse that could be from a van."

"This kid who saw Kerry yesterday," Allen said, "is he a reliable witness?"

"He better be, because he's all we've got. We're running a background check on him. Jeff Andrews. Know him?"

"No."

"In again, out again scouting. So far good school record, but no earthshaker. We'll know more from his application when we finish looking at it."

"Application?"

"Would-be cop. He's applied for our cadet program."

"Maybe that says something for him, Tony?"

"It would if he had more references. A steadier involvement in youth activities, a bit more of an employment record."

Allen said, "Not all kids are interested in what Blanton has to offer. Some are—"

"Okay," Tony interrupted him. "I know where you're going—your old diehard dream of a community center. And I'm with you there. But we still do the old routine here when we're going to talk to anyone. No matter how helpful he wants to be."

"And you're good at that," Allen said. Then he asked what he had wanted to ask from the beginning. "How is Mrs. Blake doing?"

"Of course she's shaken up. The girl has never been out of line in her life, according to the mother. That's why we're taking this seriously. But, Allen, when you were out there at the Hopper House yesterday, did you notice anything?"

"Like what?"

"A window open in the left wing."

"Yes. There was."

"Did you get down to the basement?"

"No, Tony. The old lady has a bad knee, and besides it was dark as a pocket down there."

"Damn," Tony said, a rare lapse for him.

"Why?"

"It would have helped, that's all. We don't have any bloodhound noses like yours around anymore."

"And what would I have sniffed?"

"I don't know, that's just it. But whatever, it would

have hit you fresh. By the time we got the search warrant, what we found was ancient—no recent trash, only stuff that had been accumulating there for years. Except a floor drain had apparently been used as a urinal, and we found one small dab of cigarette ash next to it. Both apparently fresh, left by whoever was just in there. And by now I'm sure convinced there was someone in there. But the place is a stink bomb of old filth, and we couldn't tell fresh from whatever."

"How did the ash test out?"

"It's legal."

"Okay, Tony. Tell me what you really want to tell me."

"A blue hair clasp. Near the bottom of the basement steps. Her mother is positive it's one Kerry has worn for years. We've also got some good footprints outside that open window and inside. They look like the kind of tennis shoes Kerry was wearing at the time. And there are others. You may have to let us look at what you had on, too. You know the routine."

"What about the bike?"

"We didn't find it."

"Not even on the grounds?"

"No. No bike."

Allen hesitated, then he said, "Look, Tony—don't think I'm gone, but there isn't anything like a secret passage—in other words, did you comb the place? Could the bike be in the house somewhere?"

"That's not as far out as you think. Those old houses have some odd holes in them, but we've been all over the place. And the realty company could only furnish an incomplete sketch of partial construction data going back to some remodeling."

"What remodeling?"

"Late fifties or early sixties—thereabouts. A fellow from Florida was going to use it for some summer house or something. Big orange-grove guy. He got himself in some trouble, and it fell through. We've put a trace on that, but I don't know at this distance in time that we can expect much."

"The only thing I noticed," Allen said, "was the bathrooms in the right wing were in better shape than the others."

"That's about as far as the remodeling went, it seems. Our main problem is that the locks on the house haven't been changed in years, and until about seven years ago there was a long series of tenants. There are probably dozens of keys floating around. The last bunch who rented out there were crazies. They were evicted. We're looking into that list, too, but . . ." He trailed off, and Allen could visualize the characteristic shrug of frustration.

"Tony, how bad is this really?"

"I can't say yet. But I don't like the way it's starting off."

"I don't suppose there is anything I can do." It was not a question, rather a statement of resignation.

"Yes, darn you. You can *think*, Allen! You were *out* there!"

There was a pause. Then Tony asked, "How well do you know Sandra Blake?"

"I just met her yesterday."

Another pause. "Allen, I wish you were still on the force."

"You know why I'm not. I didn't think I was accomplishing there what I could if I worked through council. So I ran."

"I know, I know. I voted against you, but you got it. And you're right. You've done a lot of good things. For us and the city. But, Allen, I'm going to need you."

"You tell me what you want, Chief, and I'll do my best."

"You'll be working under 'Special Assignments,' and you should know what that means, since you set it up through council. No pay. We don't have the budget to put you back on the payroll, as you well know. Can you spare the time?"

"Tony, just tell me what you want me to do."

"We're getting the usual good cooperation from Natalie Powers and the *Morning Herald*. She's put the clamps on her staff and is only releasing what we give her. But that new outfit, *The Blanton Eyes and Ears,* is being pretty pushy."

"Yes—the kids with the tabloid and radio station. I've had a few run-ins with them over council business."

"Unfortunately," Tony said, "they're waiting around like vultures on Sandra Blake's doorstep."

"They would. That's how they 'scoop.' They might as well call their sheet *The Yellow Page* and be done with it. Somebody's going to stick it to them one day."

"Maybe you should start now. There's not much the department can do other than our official 'No comment,' but maybe you can. And, Allen, I want you to get to know Sandra Blake. I think I'm going to need the Davidson touch on this."

"All I can do there, Tony, is try."

"Well, you sure have come through for me before, old buddy. Okay?"

"Okay. But if anything comes in on the girl, I want to know."

"You'll know," his old friend said. "And from you I want a lot of thought. I want your beagle nose, so go back out to that house."

When he hung up, Allen looked at his watch; he should be on his way to the office. He would make one more quick call first, and then he would go. But this was something he needed to do—wanted to do. Now. For several reasons. But it was strange how the old excitement hit him when he was back at work with Tony.

He dialed the *Morning Herald* and asked for Natalie Powers.

"Natalie," he said, "do you have a minute to talk?"

"For you, Allen, I always make time."

"Thanks. Fill me in on Sandra Blake."

Jeff Andrews had found Hopper's Lane cordoned off at both ends. He had thought that maybe if he took some time out there, put himself just where he had been when he'd seen the van, he might remember it more clearly. He knew that there was nothing definite to connect it to Kerry. Still, he had an uncanny feeling that the van figured in all this.

He had borrowed his brother's car, but when he got to the corner of Dexter and Hopper's Lane, he was stopped by the policeman on duty. After a few minutes of futile argument, during which the policeman took his name and address and made Jeff feel that he himself was suspect, he turned around and went to the service station on Dexter.

In the pay phone booth he looked up car lots and dealerships. He knew just about every maker carried vans, but he thought maybe if he saw one like that dark green van, he'd be able to pin down the make and model.

The first used-car lot he went to had no vans at all. The second had some campers, but no vans like the one he had seen. By noon he had gone to four lots, in and around the city of Blanton, and although he had seen two similar to the kind he was after, he was sure that the dark green one was somehow different.

He pulled into a McDonald's. For a few minutes he sat in the car and tried to make his mind go blank. If he could just get an image in his memory of what he had seen that late evening, if he could only picture the back of that van, maybe he could come up with something more definite than just the Minnesota tag.

He remembered that the sun was setting in a wild pinky color. Since it was late, he and Kerry had talked only a few minutes. Then—what? He had gone on toward Johnson Drive and had seen the van turning in. The lane was full of shadows, the van was dark and running without headlights. He had seen the two vague male figures in the front seat; the van had passed him and he had turned.

In the weird light of the lane, the back of the van had a bilious sort of tint to it. He had seen the tag distinctly

enough to notice the state, but what about the back of
the van itself? Well, the two vans he had seen this morning were different, but how? Something about the back.
Yes—that was it. The back of the dark green van had no
windows!

He knew that now—if it had had windows, the light
reflecting from them would have made the upper part of
the back show up differently. But the whole back had
been murky, almost purple where the fading pink light
struck the dull, dark green finish.

Suddenly he wasn't hungry anymore. He looked at his
list of lots and dealerships and checked off the ones he
had visited. That left two more, one off the north bypass,
the other out near Dudley. There was a large Ford deal-
ership there, too, so he decided to head for Dudley.

As he approached the outskirts of the suburb he saw
he was going to have a bit more luck. The Ford dealer-
ship had a large lot and there were half a dozen or so
vans parked on it. He pulled the car into a parking place,
got out, and went to the office. He wasn't sure what he
was going to say or ask and suddenly felt shy about his
mission. But a neatly dressed man with a welcoming
smile came up to him and asked if he could help.

"Yes," Jeff said. "I need to find out the make of a van
I saw that I—well, it's just important that I find out what
kind it was."

"A Ford? That's all we carry here."

"That's the problem. I'm not really sure."

"Well, why don't we go out and look at what I have.
Maybe that will help."

"You sure you're not too busy?"

"I've got a few minutes." He told his secretary that he would be outside, then led Jeff out to the lot.

There he asked, "Do you have an idea what size?"

"Sort of. Those over there are close. They have the same front end—short-nosed, but not flat."

"Those are our newer models. We stopped making that flat front about 1975."

Jeff looked closely at the row of light-colored vans. The front ends looked just like what he remembered, and he felt encouraged. Going up to the nearest one, he noted the size, then walked around it. It had rear windows. His moment of hope flickered low. The next one had windows not only in the rear, but on the sides as well.

"I don't think it's like these," he said. "The one I saw didn't have any windows except up front. None in the rear or back panel at all."

"Windows come extra," the dealer explained. "The standards just have the two front cab windows—like that one over there." He pointed to a brown van parked near the service area. "It's the short wheelbase, but you can look at it and see if this is what you mean."

They walked over to it. The more Jeff looked at the front, the surer he was that the green van was like it. He walked around to the back and his heart flipped. No windows. He could swear the rear of the van he'd seen on Hopper's Lane was like this.

"And those?" He had started back to the longer vans. "These here wouldn't have windows in the standard model?"

"Right. These longer ones are our 138-inch wheelbase. They're the most popular models. E-100 Econoline vans. Stripped down, they're just like that brown one, only longer, of course."

"What else would a standard have?"

The dealer laughed. "You mean what else *wouldn't* it have besides windows."

"Yeah. That."

"Well, for instance, there's no inside door release on the rear door. You have to get out and open it with a key from the outside. I have one like that, and it isn't very convenient."

Jeff peered in the window. "They actually look pretty much like this?"

"Yes. Same metal floor. The seats are like these. There's no other dash storage—no lock compartment. Just a slot like this for maps and things. Dome light goes on with the dash interior light. You control it with this switch."

"The dome light just over the seats like this? No light in back?"

"Inside? No. Just this one."

Jeff's excitement was mounting. "You sell them all over the country?"

The dealer looked at him with amusement. "Yes, indeed! They're a big item. How about you? Can I sell you one?"

"Not today." Jeff felt the warmth of urgency in his face. "But I'd like to borrow your phone."

"Help yourself." He waved toward the office. "It's on my desk. Just tell my secretary I said it's okay."

Jeff was already on his way. Then he turned. "Hey—thanks a lot!"

He didn't hear the dealer chuckling to himself. Jeff had what he wanted now, and he needed to report in.

9

Sandra was lying down when the doorbell rang. The bedside clock showed five, the hands painfully slow to mark off a long afternoon after an endless night and morning of waiting for word of Kerry. She hurriedly slipped on her shoes and ran to the door; Chief Perez had promised to keep her informed of any developments.

Some of her old friends from across town had come earlier, sympathetic but uneasy with their proffered help, as if this new unhappy event in Sandra's widowhood had set her even farther apart from their comfortable normal lives. She had not seen many of them since Ted's funeral, had deliberately cut herself off from them to escape their strained friendship, to avoid being reminded of the happy times they had all shared together. She had accepted their tentative "Call me if there is anything I can do" and let them slide out of her life again. Now she hoped this would be some hope she could cling to that Kerry was all right.

But when she opened the door, it was not a policeman. Allen Davidson stood on the little stoop in the fall afternoon light.

"May I come in?" he asked.

She had stood with the door held open, surprised; then she stepped back into the sitting room. He came in, and she shut the door.

Sandra found herself looking at him as if for the first time. Yesterday she had been so completely undone that she had hardly seen him. Now she was aware of refined features, the shock of thick brown hair, the graying temples. Everything about him spelled steadiness and good sense.

He was not really a tall man, but he looked tall in the middle of the small room. He stood there as if he had been here, just like this, many times before. There was a gentleness about his face. His brown eyes looked at her with such concern that, for the first time, she felt as if the tremendous loneliness of her vigil would get the better of her. Her throat clamped against a cry as she tried to stifle her anguish before she gave way completely. And then, before she knew what was happening, she was in this man's arms, sobbing against his shoulder as he cradled her head against him, holding her close, letting her cry out her need and her fear.

Struggling desperately to regain control, she moved away and sat in the chair beside the couch. "Thank you," she said. "It—it's been a very long twenty-four hours."

"I know." He sat down too. "Sandra, I didn't know you were Ted Blake's wife."

She looked up over her handkerchief. The mention of his name brought Ted closer to her, brought him into the moment almost as if his presence were tangibly with them, and she was grateful.

"You knew Ted?"

"I met him one day last spring. He was having lunch with Larry English. Larry and I are old friends."

She nodded. "I'm so glad you knew him."

"Larry thought a great deal of Ted. I wish I had known him well."

She swallowed and blew her nose quietly. "Yes," she said. She sat with her handkerchief pressed to her lips, fighting to stay in control. Then she nodded, unable to say more.

"I've been in touch with Tony Perez. He and I were in school together and have known each other since, in many capacities. Including police work."

A total panic rose in Sandra's heart, so forcefully that she started up from the couch.

"No—" Allen reached out a hand. "I should have made it clear from the first. I'm not bringing you bad news. Actually there isn't any more than what you already know except that the kid who saw Kerry on Hopper's Lane thinks he now knows the make of the van. Tony has put Grady Potts in charge of investigation. He's a good man."

"Jeff Andrews—yes, Jeff came by. I guess he's really the best friend Kerry's got. Such a nice boy—so concerned—wanting to be helpful."

"Tony says he may have given us our big break if that van is found and if Grady Potts can find anything to connect it to Kerry."

Us, she thought. Yes. He's in this too. I knew he was the minute he walked in that door.

She said, "I'm afraid I got your coat all wet."

He glanced down and smiled. "So you did. Did it help?"

"Yes. Tremendously."

"Why don't you accept Natalie's offer to stay over here with you at night?"

"I—I do better by myself. It's a small apartment. She wouldn't be very comfortable."

"She'd like to come. It's obvious I've talked to her about you. Look. You shouldn't wall yourself off at a time like this."

She stood up. "Would you like something—a cup of tea—a drink?"

"I'd like the tea, unless you're having something stronger." He followed her out to the little kitchen. "Really, let Natalie come over."

She set a bottle of gin on the side of the sink and faced him. "This may come as a surprise to you after I cried on your shoulder, but I—"

He waited. She could only turn away as tears welled up again.

"The shoulder is still available," he said.

She shook her head. "I'll be all right in a minute. It's just that—once the dam breaks, it floods."

She felt his hands on her shoulders, felt him turn her around to face him. It would be so easy to give way again, to cling to him, to let him shelter her again in his arms. But then he would be gone, and she would be utterly alone again, more alone even than if he had not come. No. It was better just to stand on her own two feet.

She wiped her eyes and gave him a shaky smile. "I don't have anything very exciting to put in this drink. Does gin and Coke sound ghastly?"

"It's been done, I think, in the very best of places."

"And I can't find my jigger."

He took the bottle from her and poured a small measure in each glass. She handed him the ice tray and a cold Coke, the Coke she had saved for Kerry. Tears surged up dangerously again and she choked them back.

She said thickly, "It's not really any use—I don't do a very good job of pretending. I think that's why I don't want anyone over here with me. I would feel I had to bear up, and there are times when I just can't."

"I think Natalie would understand that."

"Yes. Natalie is a good friend, but even friends make me want to put on a good face." She felt herself flush. "I only bawl all over perfect strangers."

"Let's sit down a minute, shall we?"

They went back to the sitting room and Sandra sat again on the chair. Allen sat on the couch and put his drink on the coffee table.

He said, "Would you let a perfect stranger take you out for supper? I can call in to Tony and let him know where we'll be."

"I'm really not hungry."

"I know. We'll get something light. You need to eat."

The warm brown eyes were completely frank. A stranger, she thought. But she wondered if Allen Davidson was ever a stranger to anyone. No wonder Natalie thought so highly of him. He was a thoroughly nice person.

She nodded. "Yes. I would like to go."

"Good. While you get ready I'll call Tony. We won't stay out long."

In her bedroom she saw herself in the mirror. Her face was blotchy from crying, her eyes red, with circles under them. But somehow it just didn't matter. She would sponge her face with cold water, do what she could to restore herself, but Allen Davidson would understand.

The knot in her heart began to ease a little. For an hour or so she would not be alone. She would be with a comfortable person whose compassion, too, was comfortable. He was the only person since Ted had died who felt free to mention Ted's name in her presence, felt no difficulty in talking about him. Everyone seemed so ill at ease with her grief, so reluctant to bring him into the conversation that this, as much as anything, had made her leave it all behind.

But Allen Davidson was at home with the thought and the memory of Ted. And his genuine concern had a completely practical quality to it. She felt there was no danger he would be oversolicitous, which would only add to her burden. He would make no demands on her fragile endurance. She could trust him to be the friend she needed for just this hour.

When the van stopped, Carl jerked awake. He had no idea how long he had been asleep. Now he stared at the strange, dingy motel. So Ax had finally got tired; he had driven straight through. Carl supposed it must now be at least three in the morning.

"Isn't this risky?" Carl asked.

"No. Jerry is a friend of mine. He's expecting me."

As Carl looked at Ax something in the back of his mind began to take shape, a suspicion he had not found enough evidence to support before. All right. Ax had known Benny was coming to that old house back in Blanton. He had known Benny was after a big pickup. He had meant to get it out of Benny. And then what? What had he meant to do with Benny then? And with him, Carl? If that girl hadn't come along and shaken up Ax's plans, just where would he be now? Double-crossed and dead? He could read nothing in the man's impassive face.

Ax said, "Go in the office. Tell Jerry I'm here."

For a second Carl hesitated. "What," he thought, "if I refused? Ax would just as soon as not shoot me in the back as I go in that door, and a friend of his would take it in stride. I'm cornered, and I don't like it. I don't like it at all. All I can do is play along until something develops I can use. One way or the other." He got out of the van.

In the small, stuffy office Carl delivered the message to the man at the counter. Surprise flickered in the man's eyes so briefly that Carl was not even sure he had seen it. The man was not expecting him? In that case Ax had meant to get rid of him along with Benny, collect Carl's share of the payoff, too, as well as what Benny was after. Maybe leave them both behind in that old house and to hell with the guys who were to take the stuff he and Ax had brought there. Ax would figure to have got his by then.

The man, Jerry, gave Carl two sets of keys. Carl looked at them. All the while Jerry was watching him closely. Carl could feel the little slant eyes boring into his mind, see the questions forming there.

Carl said, "Thanks," and went back out to the van. He handed Ax the keys. "What now?"

"Get in. The room's around back. Jerry saves it for me—it's hidden from the road and from most of the other rooms."

Carl got in. "What are the other keys?"

"A car."

The questions in Carl's mind began to bump against one inescapable fact: Ax had this planned down to the last detail. And Carl had not been included in that design. Ax had meant to get rid of him all the time. Carl had got himself into something way over his head, and he couldn't be sure he would ever get out of it, much less ever get his share.

He had heard about Ax's kind. Contacts. In stir and out. Everywhere contacts to give him tips, like Benny being in that house after something so valuable that Ax would risk everything to get it. And people like Jerry planted all along the way with rooms and cars and extra gas, everything he needed to shake a tail, if there was one. And maybe there wouldn't be one now, except that girl got mixed up in it. What was Ax going to do with her? Ransom her? Maybe he was stopping here so he could find out from her how much she was worth. She couldn't very well answer questions with a gag in her mouth.

They parked in front of a room in deep shadows. It was quiet back there, away from the road.

Ax said, "Get in back and untie them."

Carl got out and opened the back of the van. He climbed in, shoved the canvas aside, moved the bike out of the way, and by the dim light from the dome, started to untie the ropes. "What about the gags?"

"Those too." Ax leaned over the back of the seat. "Now listen to me," he said. "We're going in that room. You, girl, and Benny will walk in front of Carl, and I'll be right behind you with this leveled at you." He held Benny's .38 in his hand.

Carl could see Ax putting the revolvers they had brought into the van's toolbox. He heard him lock it.

Ax waited until the last rope was removed before he slid out of the van. "All right," he said. "Just do what I told you."

Carl said, "I'll need to unlock."

"No. It's already open. Jerry has checked it out to be sure. Just go on in."

"So," Carl thought, "I'm no better off than the girl or Benny."

The room was small, and Carl could smell the mildew as they entered. There were two lumpy single beds and a cubicle of a bathroom that smelled dirty. Behind him Carl heard Ax close and lock the door. He used the key Jerry had given him. The windows were curtained so that the light Ax had switched on would show nothing from inside.

"This is no ordinary motel room," Carl thought. "It's a perfect hideaway." He tried not to let anything show in his face or in his actions. Ax must go on thinking him a stupid hulk ready to do his bidding and too thick to know what was going on. That was his only chance.

"How long we going to stay here?" Carl asked.

"I'm going to get some sleep," Ax answered. He went into the bathroom and shut the door. From inside he said, "I'll be out in a little while. But just remember—I have the only key to this room, and Jerry will be watching everything that goes on."

Carl looked at Benny and the girl. She sat stiffly on the edge of one of the beds, the mattress sagging. Carl could see the red places on her wrists and ankles from the ropes.

She hadn't said anything since he took the gag off. She looked white as a sheet and bone-tired. He was surprised that she sat on the bed. When she had first come into the room and stood there looking around, he saw panic on her chalky face. She had looked at the beds, and he knew what must be going through her mind. He had no idea what kind of guy Ax was with women, or Benny either for that matter. But as far as he was concerned, there had better not be any funny business with this girl. He didn't want any more raps heaped up in case they got caught.

Benny's eyes held a silent question. Carl knew what he was wondering, but made his own face a blank. Whatever was going to happen to Benny was going to happen, so he needn't look at Carl in that hopeful way. Carl had nothing to do with Benny. Or the girl. Carl's only concern was Carl, and right now he was thinking ahead of this moment. He was thinking that some way, he didn't know how, he was going to get out of this. Alive. And whatever happened to Benny or the girl was their own affair. He had nothing to do with them at all. Nothing.

—————— 10 ——————

Kerry scarcely distinguished between the rest of that miserable night and the day that followed. Locked in the motel, time was marked by Jerry bringing food or other things. The heavy curtains remained closed. There was nothing to look at except the others. Three men. Well, two men and a boy. Long ugly silences hung like the curtains covering the day outside.

So she watched the others. Ax and Benny and Carl ate the things on the greasy tray, but Kerry found even the smell revolting. It mingled with the filthy odor of the bathroom, the stale smoke of Ax's endless cigarettes, the musty dirtiness of the whole place. She ate a few pieces of bread, drank some milk; nothing else would go down.

Benny needed to wipe his chin. Ax chewed with his mouth open—maybe because of the scar. So she watched the boy—Carl.

She watched how he ate. He never looked up or spoke, but he wasn't offensive. She looked at his big hands, saw their stained roughness. A workman's hands. But he couldn't be a workman. He would be in school. He didn't look any older than she was. Then why was he here?

His face was rugged, the end of his stubby nose reddish from too many peelings. She couldn't see his eyes because he wouldn't look at her either. But his eyebrows were bleached, like his blond hair, except near the bottoms, where they were heavy and nearly brown. The growth on his cheeks and chin had been brown until he used the razor Jerry brought. She remembered a boy at her old school who was always blond in summer and a redhead in winter. He played tennis.

She looked at Carl's clothes. He probably got them at a tall-shop outlet. His denim jacket was faded from many washings. The lining was plaid flannel, and sweat stains by the armholes had set.

She saw Ax look at his watch.

Jerry came and took the tray away.

Night again.

Ax ordered her and Benny to lie on the floor once more between the twin beds. She heard Ax stretch out, saw the red glow of his cigarette as he smoked in the darkness. Carl shifted about restlessly on the other bed. A flare of the cigarette lighter again. She supposed Ax was making up for the long time in the van when he didn't dare light up because of the extra gas they carried. Finally she heard him stub out what she hoped would be his last one. Then he began to snore.

The floor was hard under the thin dusty rug. Several times she felt Benny's arm touching her, his fat flesh warm and repulsive. She moved away until she was almost under Carl's bed.

She didn't know how long she had been like that before she began to shiver so hard her teeth chattered uncontrollably.

"Shut up," Ax growled and turned over noisily.

But she couldn't stop shaking.

In the narrow bed above her Carl tossed about. A few minutes later she felt the blanket from his bed slide down beside her. She waited, not daring to pull it over her, not knowing if he were awake or asleep, or if he would snatch it back for himself. But the blanket remained there in a heap beside her. Then she felt it being shoved toward her, heard Carl turn away again, and she slowly covered herself. She was careful not to let Benny know what she was doing; she was afraid he would try to get under it with her.

She was very tired, but there was no sleep for her. She thought about her mother, about her worry and loneliness while she waited for some word. And would there ever be any word? What clue had been left behind to tell the police that Ax and Carl and Benny had been in that house? Would the car that passed the van on Hopper's Lane have noticed it? Would they have reported it?

The only sounds in the cold mustiness were Ax's snoring, Benny's wheezing, and the dripping of a faucet in the bathroom. Every now and then Carl turned over and the bed creaked and he sighed. What was he thinking about? she wondered. He didn't seem to be able to sleep either.

She moved her watch close to her ear to listen to its familiar ticking, to try to blot out the other noises, to pretend she was safe at home in her own bed. Once she must have drifted into a light, troubled sleep, because she jerked awake from a terrible dream, thinking Benny was looming over her, looking down at her like an animal. But he hadn't moved.

Suddenly there was a soft knocking on the door, and she heard Ax wake up with a snort. He switched on the light between the beds, then went to the door and unlocked it. There was a muffled conversation Kerry couldn't understand except that the tone of it seemed urgent. She assumed it must be the man Jerry, Ax's friend. In a few minutes Ax closed and locked the door again and went back to his bed. He sat on the side of it, his feet next to Kerry on the thin rug. Gray, ugly, veined feet with thick yellow broken toenails.

Benny sat on the floor next to her, a wheezing Buddha in the drab circle of light. Ax was looking at Benny, a look of such hatred that Kerry froze. And all the time Ax was looking at Benny, he was rubbing his hand slowly over the crooked scar on his face. The tension between the two men seemed like a line drawn from one to the other, a brittle line of thoughts and feelings Kerry could not even guess at. But hatred and fear hung in the air, and times past when the two men knew each other.

Benny blurted, "I didn't do that to you, Ax!"

Ax was still rubbing the scar. "No." It was almost a whisper. "But you were there, Benny. You let it happen, remember? You could have stopped it, but you didn't. You ran out on me, Benny, ran out and ratted and left me lying there with my face opened up like a can of beans. You say you didn't do it, Benny? You could have stopped it."

"No, Ax!" His voice rose. "He would have got me too! I couldn't have done anything!"

"You knew he got that hatchet. You saw him make it, and you knew he was after me. You were there on the stairway, you saw him come at me."

"So did all the others! The guards were there! I thought they would stop him!"

"You think those hacks would have stopped him? He *owned* them. But you, Benny—you *knew* there was a contract out on me. Evans told me you knew."

"No!"

"For twelve years now I've had to live with this face. And for twelve years I've been waiting to get you."

There was deadly silence. Benny's face was gray and wet with perspiration even though it was cold in the room. His eyes were wide with a stupid kind of blank pleading. Ax looked at him, and it seemed to Kerry that the scar had grown uglier as he relived the time of the prison attack.

Finally Benny said, "What are you going to do, Ax?" and his voice trembled.

"Jerry says there's an alert out for a green Econoline 100 van with a Minnesota tag. And they're looking for the girl and her bicycle. They're going to find the van, Benny. With you in it."

Kerry's heart lurched.

"We're going to drive out from here," Ax said. "I know a place where I can get rid of everything that might connect me to Blanton, Georgia. Jerry will follow us in the car."

The tension she had felt earlier became unbearable. It was not just between Ax and Benny now. It was between all of them.

"Get up," Ax said.

Kerry stood up, clutching the blanket in front of her as if it could shield her from the look on Ax's face, make her invisible behind its dingy brown. She could feel her heart pumping, her hands shaking. Benny had stumbled to his feet. Carl was standing, too, slowly tucking in his shirt, not saying anything, not looking at any of them. Then slowly he put on his jacket. Everything slowly, like a held breath. There was nothing in Carl's face to give her a hint of his feelings or thoughts. But what would he be feeling now, anyway? Why should he care about what was going to happen to her or Benny?

Ax had finished putting on his shoes. "We're going to get in the van," he said. "Jerry will be right behind us."

He unlocked the door of the room and waited while they filed past him. The night was still dark. It was cold and overcast with a dampness that cut through Kerry's sweatshirt. She could see the other car, dim in the darkness, the blurred outline of someone inside. Ax transferred two guns out of the toolbox under the driver's seat of the van to Jerry's waiting car. Carl unlocked the back of the van.

Ax said, "Carl, put those fuel cans in the room. I'll lock up."

Silently Carl obeyed.

Then Ax said, "Get in. No need to tie them, Carl. It's not far. Just cover them and the bike."

Kerry and Benny lay down on the floor of the van again. Carl put the bike down on top of them and covered them with the canvas. Then he got into the front of the van. Kerry heard the other car start up, then the van engine. There was no need to think about signaling with the headlight now. No one would see it but Jerry.

As the van moved steadily away from the motel Kerry's fingernails dug into the palms of her hands. Her teeth were clamped tight over a scream she would not scream.

Ax was going to get rid of Benny and the van. He needed to get rid of her and her bike too. What was he planning to do with them?

She closed her eyes and prayed.

The piercing ring of the telephone brought Sandra fumbling from a shallow sleep, grasping for the receiver. She could see dimly by the light she had left on in the living room. Even as she was saying "Hello" a tangle of thoughts churned her mind—was it Kerry—was it the ransom call Detective Potts said might come—was it . . . ?

"Hello!" she said again. She reached for the pad and

pencil on the bedside table, ready to write down information, anything at all. "Hello!"

But no one spoke. She could hear breathing on the other end of the line. She had been warned about possible crank calls. But suppose this was Kerry, unable to speak?

"Hello?" Sandra said again.

Then the stealthy sound of a receiver being replaced. The dial tone droned into the silence that followed.

Sandra put the phone back on the table and switched on the bedside lamp. She waited a few minutes. Maybe it *was* a ransom call, and something had happened to keep the caller from speaking. Maybe whoever it was would call back. She looked at the clock. Four thirty. What should she do? She couldn't tie up the line by trying to get the police. Besides, maybe it was a wrong number. No. Nobody would do that in the dead of night without at least saying "I'm sorry."

She got up and drew on her robe. Pacing, she walked the little space between the bed and the window, her hands clasped together in front of her.

Suddenly the phone split the silence again, and she leapt for it.

"Hello!" she said. But again there was no answer. "Please!" she begged. "Hello! Is anyone there?"

Again only the breathing came to her over the line. Then the other person hung up.

Sandra stared down at the phone in anguish. How could anyone do this—this cruel, inhuman thing? What was the point? What satisfaction could someone get from torturing a mother whose daughter was missing? Was it the kidnapper, toying with her, manipulating her so that she would accept whatever ungodly sum was required to get Kerry back safely?

She covered her eyes with her hands.

"Oh, Ted," she thought. "I need you! I am so alone."

And the phone rang again. Again there was no sound but the breathing.

"Please don't do this," she said, and put the receiver back on the hook. To the room she said, "Don't do that to me anymore. I can't take it."

And the telephone rang again. She let it ring. When it stopped, she called the police.

Carl was acutely aware of every sound now, everything in sight, as the van moved steadily away from the motel. Nothing escaped his mental note, nothing the van passed, no tree, no house; no dog barked in the distance without becoming part of a picture so clear in his mind he would never forget it. He knew every position of the van in relation to the motel, an empty filling station, a pasture with a broken, rotting barbed-wire fence, a crossroads that led to an even more remote section of the countryside. All were indelibly placed in the computer of his mind so that he would have total recall when he needed it.

This was much better than thrashing around in that motel bed, wondering what was going to happen and when. It was almost as if he were on speed; taut, brittle, with a feeling of intense aliveness born of a desperate need to form some sort of plan to get himself out of this. Because he had no doubt now about what Ax meant to do. Ax would fix a scene getting rid of everything that could possibly link him to the stash in Blanton and the disappearance of the girl. And Carl was as dangerous to Ax now as the girl and Benny were.

Carl pictured how it would be. The cops had an alert out for the girl and the van. Ax would set up the perfect ditch by putting the girl and her bike in the back of the van, Carl and Benny in the front, and somehow push them all into some kind of smashup. Then, when the cops found the van and its occupants, they would think the case was solved. That would leave Ax home free to pick up his share, and Carl's, too, and go on to the next job. "Oh, how smooth," Carl thought.

His spun-out high felt good. He felt indomitable. Indestructible. There was no way Ax could double-cross him because he knew it was coming.

And now the van was bumping over a rutted gravel road; they must be about fifteen miles from the motel, Carl thought. They had followed a river the last few miles, had bumped over a single railroad track and crossed a bridge. Now the van headed up an incline where rocks stuck out of the ground on all sides. At the top of the steep slope the van slowed down, and Carl could see a black area spread out down a sharp drop: more outcropping of rock, and stones, and the sound of water moving below.

Ax pulled the van to a stop. "This is it," he said.

"What is it?" Carl asked.

"An old rock quarry. Not used anymore."

Oh, perfect, Carl thought. The van loaded with everything Ax needed to get rid of would go over the bank and out of sight.

"Get them out of the back and over to Jerry's car," Ax said. "I've got some fixing to do."

Carl opened the back of the van, pulled the canvas and bike off the girl and Benny, and stood aside while they got out. In the dim light that filtered back from the cab of the van, Carl saw with a shock of awareness how white the girl was. She had dirty smudges under her eyes, as if she had been crying. But he hadn't heard a sound out of her. He wished he hadn't looked at her. It was too bad she got mixed up in all this, but he could not think about that now.

Jerry was parked just a few feet back, sitting in the driver's seat. The girl got in the backseat of the car. Carl saw her ball up like she had a stomachache. On the front seat he could see the two guns Ax had transferred from the van, black shapes next to Jerry's thigh.

Benny stood outside the car next to Carl, on the side away from Jerry, and he was quiet. Even his wheezing wasn't so loud. The night was still, with only the slurping sound of water in the gravel pit.

Suddenly the sound of splintering glass shattered the quiet. Pounding the front end of the van with a rock, Ax smashed the windshield, bringing the rock against it over and over, pounding the glass like it was alive, like it was Benny's head, or Carl's, or the girl's. He smashed the grill, and the pieces that flew off he threw down into the pit, where they made a muffled swallowing splash in the blackness.

The girl was balled up tighter now, her hands over her ears, and Carl saw her shaking the way she had back in the motel. Benny shifted his weight, and his arm brushed Carl's. Then Benny's fingers moved to Carl's hand—out of sight of Jerry and the girl. Ax was too busy with the van to see Benny press something small and flat into Carl's hand. Then Benny shifted away again.

Carl was afraid to look down at his hand or at Benny. He didn't know why, but he felt this was something strictly between the two of them. That Benny had meant it that way. Beside him Benny sighed, as if he were relieved. Or resigned. Carl slid his hand into his pocket, putting the thing Benny had given him down deep inside. It felt like a small piece of thin cardboard.

Ax finished with the van and walked toward the car. He stood facing Benny, his breath coming hard, the dim light hovering in the jagged crease of the scar. The battered front end of the van perched on the edge of the gravel pit.

"Put the Minnesota tag on it, Carl," Ax said. "Put the box with the other plates in the car."

Inside the van were the canvas, the ropes, the box of plates, and the girl's bike. Carl changed the tag, taking the tools and plates to the car.

"All right," Ax said. He pulled Benny's .38 out of his belt and pointed it at Benny's belly. "Come here, Benny. I've wiped the wheel and the inside of the cab. Now I want your prints on it. Move."

Benny got into the van. The door stood open, and Carl could see his fat bulk under the steering wheel, his face turned back toward Ax.

"Put your hands on the wheel," Ax said. "I want lots of prints." Then he chuckled. "That's good. Very good."

The girl suddenly sat up in the back of the car. "Please," she cried, "I need to get out! I'm going to be sick! Please let me go over there—" She pointed to the scrub growth at the edge of the road.

Ax didn't even look back at her. "Go ahead then," he said. He held the muzzle of the gun in his hand, the butt extended like a bludgeon. He said, "Lean your head out here, Benny. Farther. Oh, that's nice. That's perfect."

Carl closed his eyes. He heard the thudding sounds, and when they stopped, he looked, and Benny was sprawled at Ax's feet.

"Put him back in the van, Carl."

Ax was standing over Benny, the butt of the gun still protruding from his hand. As Carl squatted beside the unconscious Benny he could feel Ax's sharp, hard breath close against his shoulder.

Suddenly Carl saw his chance. From a crouch he sprang against Ax, at the same time grabbing the butt of the gun. It was like lightning. Ax was flat on his back and Carl had the .38—he whirled and fired wildly, point-blank at the windshield of the car, drilling it where he hoped Jerry's head would be.

On the ground Ax grabbed Carl's legs. Carl went down, his gun hand pinned to the ground by Ax's claw-like grip. Carl was working by instinct now, animal reflex that told him Ax was much stronger than he had guessed, strong with a wiry strength and trained in every dirty trick Carl had ever heard of.

For a moment the two were almost motionless as Ax's fingers cut into Carl's straining wrist. Then with a quick thrust of his full weight, Carl wrenched loose, but Ax's knee was already driving with all its force into Carl's groin.

In spite of the lightning pain that pierced him, Carl somehow managed to hang onto the gun. Nausea gripped him. He heard Ax's feet pounding the gravel as he raced to the car, and Carl knew he was after the two revolvers on the seat.

With the white-hot pain searing him, Carl forced himself up and made a lunge at the row of bushes beside the road, the .38 tight in his hand. He rolled out of sight of the car and began working his way down the face of the quarry, feeling, clutching the rocks of the pit until he reached the shelter of an overhang that protected him from above. He wedged himself into a small fissure, flattened himself in the little cave, afraid even to breathe. Pebbles fell down and splashed below as Ax paced overhead, looking for him.

The pain was now a dull throbbing inside him, and Carl gripped the rock face, pressing his forehead against its coldness. After a few minutes he heard another flurry of motion above, then shots. Three of them. A few more minutes. The car door slammed. The engine started, and gravel sprayed as the car started off.

Carl waited. The sound of tires and motor grew fainter and fainter.

He closed his eyes. The pain and nausea were unbearable. When he opened his eyes again, he saw a dim rim of daylight coming over the edge of the pit. The ledge where he was crouching was pocked with other fissures like the one he was in. And not far from him was the girl—her fingers clinging to the rocks, her face a mask of terror.

11

Kerry dared not move. She stared at Carl across the face of the ledge, at the gun in his hand pointed directly at her. Seconds stretched into minutes, and she wasn't sure she could hang on any longer.

It seemed like a long time before she saw the nose of the gun slowly turn away from her. Still she didn't dare move. Then she heard stones hitting the dark water below as Carl twisted out of his small cave. He tucked the gun in his belt and started climbing slowly back up the sheer face of the rock, his feet searching for footholds.

She watched his progress fearfully, not knowing what he was going to do. At last he hunched himself over the last outcrop and disappeared behind the lip of the cliff on top.

She waited, her heart pounding. Below her the dark, murky water was ringed where dislodged stones continued to fall. Holding her breath, she listened for sounds of movement above, but heard nothing. She waited until she thought there had been plenty of time for Carl to get away. Then she began to climb carefully up the ledge. Slipping and grasping, she finally managed to pull herself all the way to the top and onto level ground.

She froze. There was Carl, sitting against a boulder, the gun in his hand. He sat very still, his face white under streaks of dirt, his blond hair matted now and stuck to his forehead.

In the deadly quiet Kerry could hear her own labored breathing. She and Carl were walled off from the van by the line of scrub growth. She listened, but there was no sound from over there.

She stared at the black hole of the gun muzzle, then at Carl. But he didn't get up.

"Did they shoot you?" she asked.

After a pause he answered, "He might as well have."

Kerry's scraped and bleeding hands smarted, her jeans were torn. But all she could think of was Carl and the gun.

"Well," she cried, "what are you going to do? Are you going to shoot me?"

Without answering, he got slowly to his feet. He seemed very big standing over her, the gun in his hand. Then he turned away and spread the bushes, peering through toward the van. Moving slowly, he edged through the brush; the branches closed behind him. She could barely see beyond the thicket, could barely follow his movements as he walked cautiously toward the van, the gun in front of him. She remembered hearing the sound of shots and the car motor earlier, and now she didn't know what might be over there.

Kerry squatted down and looked all around her. She wanted to find some way out of there while Carl was over by the van. But there was none. If she left the safety of the scrub growth, the only way she could go was past the van. There was nothing to do but wait where she was. Carl had not shot her. Maybe he would just leave her there, and she would be safe to find her way out, back to civilization and a telephone.

Gnats gathered about her head and she brushed them away. She looked for a tree big enough to have moss on it. She had always heard that moss grew on the north side, and maybe that way she could get a hint of which direction was which. She had no idea where she was, not even which state she was in. The sun was coming up fast, and she got a general sense of where east was, but the sun had such seasonal angles that she didn't trust it alone for bearings.

After waiting for what seemed a long time, she looked through the bushes to see if Carl had gone. She knew he couldn't go in the van since there was a lookout for it, and Ax must have ruined it when he smashed the front end. But what she couldn't be sure of was what he planned to do with her.

He was still there. He was doing something beside the van; she couldn't tell exactly what because his back was to her, but he was kneeling down, bending over something. Then he straightened up and tossed something away. He put the gun back in his belt and looked all around—at the sky, down the gravel road that led up to the quarry, back at the van. Then he started walking down the slope, his footsteps making a chewing sound on the gravel as he disappeared around a curve. Kerry let out a long breath of relief.

She eased from behind the bushes and slowly and carefully made her way to the van. The back end was still open, and she saw her bike inside. But as she moved nearer, she stopped. Benny was lying on the ground, and she knew he was dead. She remembered the shots in the night, and closed her eyes as sickness swept over her once more. She knew Ax had killed him.

When she looked again, she saw Benny's wallet a few feet from him—open as if it had been rifled and thrown aside.

Concentrating now on getting her bike out, she forced herself not to look at Benny anymore. But when she saw her bike up close, tears of anger welled in her eyes. The back tire was slashed open. The van tires, too, were gaping. Was that what Carl was doing over here just now? But he could have taken her bike, stripped it, and ridden out of here a lot faster than he could walk. And if he had a knife all that time, if he knew all that time what Ax was going to try to do to him, wouldn't he have used it while Ax slept there in the motel?

No. Carl didn't do that to those tires.

She stumbled away and started down the crumbling road that led from the quarry. As she walked, the wrench at having to leave her bicycle became unbearable. The hate she had felt earlier for Ax mounted to a point of frenzy, and all she could think of was getting to help in time to set the alarm out for him.

At ten o'clock on the dot Jeff Andrews was ushered into the office where Detective Grady M. Potts, Criminal Investigation Division of the Blanton Police Department, waited for him. Detective Potts was a big man with a holstered service revolver on his hip. A recording device lay in an obvious position on his desk; a portable radio like the walkie-talkie Jeff and his brother used to have was beside it.

"Sit down," Potts said.

Jeff sat in the single straight chair facing the desk. Outside, the morning sun slid in and out of heavy clouds, bright rays falling across the mess of folders and papers on top of the desk—a mess, and yet neat somehow, Jeff observed.

Potts said, "I called you in because Chief Perez says you've telephoned several times about the Kerry Blake case."

"Yes, sir," Jeff said.

"You're sure about the make of the van?"

"Yes, sir. As sure as I can be. I looked at every kind of van made, just about, and the Econoline 100 base-model cargo van is at least close. I think that's the kind I saw."

"What makes you so sure the van is involved in the first place?"

"Well, sir, I've been running out that way for a while now. You know it's pretty remote, and, well, there just never had been any cars or trucks on that road before. I mean while I was running there."

"Can you describe any occupants?"

"No, sir. Except that there were two males. At least that's all I saw."

Potts waited.

Then Jeff added, uncertainly, "The guy driving looked smaller than the other one."

"You saw two males, then," Potts said. "That's all you're sure of."

"Yes, sir. I'm positive they weren't women or girls."

"Or men with wigs?"

"No. Short hair."

"How short?"

"About—well, about regular length."

"Tag number?"

"I didn't get the number." Jeff could see all this written there in the report, even looking at it upside down from where he sat. But he added, "Minnesota. I saw that."

"And Kerry Blake? You saw her"—and here Potts looked at the notes—"about three thirty in the afternoon. What was she doing out there?"

"She used the lane for a shortcut home from school. She had to ride her bike to school because she's on the basketball team and the buses always leave before practice is over. I used to meet her out there sometimes."

"Three thirty—looks like she could have taken a bus."

"We didn't know there was going to be a teachers' meeting called. Nobody knew it. They canceled everything after school, including practices. She had ridden her bike to school that morning, so she rode it home."

"Were these the only times you saw her—out on Hopper's Lane when you met her there?"

"No, sir. We saw each other at school. And we went out some."

Potts was looking at the report again. "It says here you were sure she was going up to the Hopper House, that she might even go inside sometime. Why did you think that?"

"Well, she generally beat me getting there on the days I ran out that way, and she used to sit opposite the house and just stare at it. Really stare. I told her she shouldn't hang around a deserted place like that—she couldn't know who might be in it. But she thought it was, well, she said sort of romantic. The house, I mean."

"Why did you worry about her being out there alone?"

Jeff shrugged. "I just thought it wasn't such a good idea."

"Yet you'd never seen anyone on that lane? In the time you'd been running out there—except Kerry Blake. And the two males in the van?"

"No, sir."

"But it says here you saw another car on that lane, not long after you say you saw the van."

"Well, another one did turn in, yes, sir."

"But you don't think that car had anything to do with Kerry Blake?"

Jeff looked at the detective blankly for a moment. "Well, no, sir."

"Why?"

After a few uncomfortable seconds Jeff said, "Well, I don't know why. I just felt the other car was okay."

Detective Potts studied him, frowning. "And as it turns out, the car *was* okay. It was a Mrs. Murdoch, who had legitimate business there. But I want to know why you felt so strongly that it was okay for the car to be there and not the van."

Shifting in the chair, Jeff shook his head. "I can't say, sir. Call it a hunch." He thought a minute. "The van was running without headlights, and it was getting pretty dark. The car had lights on. Maybe that's why I felt like that."

"I see." Potts leaned back and locked his hands behind his head. He was a heavyset man with a grandfatherly kind face. Even his voice was gentle as he said, "Let me get this straight. You saw the van on Hopper's Lane which day?"

"The day before I heard Kerry was missing. Very late afternoon."

"And Kerry Blake was out there then too."

"She left before the van turned in. And before the car, too."

"Then tell me exactly what happened the day you saw her last."

"It was the next day. The day after I'd seen the van.

We got out of school early because of that teachers' meeting."

Potts was looking at him intently. The silence grew until Jeff felt he must say something.

"We hadn't planned to meet there that day. I just decided to go out there because I knew she would be passing that way on her way home."

"Was that when you knew she was going to try to go up to the Hopper House?"

"Well—then, and before. She really liked that old place."

"Have you ever been inside the house yourself?"

"No, sir."

"What time did you leave her after you saw her that last time?"

"I just stayed a few minutes. I—well, I had to go home."

For a tiny second Jeff thought he saw the flicker of a frown on the detective's face, but he couldn't be sure. For one thing, the big man's next question wiped everything else out.

"How well do you *really* know Kerry Blake?"

"I—well, we're friends." Jeff knew he was red as a beet, and he wished he could open a window.

Potts picked up a tagged envelope and carefully shook out a small object on a clean sheet of paper. It was a blue hair clasp. Kerry's blue butterfly hair clasp that was always coming half loose. Jeff stared at it.

Potts asked, "Have you ever seen this before?"

Jeff swallowed and nodded. "Yes, sir. It's Kerry's."

"I'm going to ask you a very important question, and I want you to think before you answer. Was she wearing this the last time you saw her?"

Jeff closed his eyes because Potts was looking at him so hard he felt suddenly weak. "Yes, sir."

"And think before you answer this. Did she, at any time, ever mention meeting anyone else out there on Hopper's Lane?"

Jeff's eyes flew open, but Potts held up his hand.

"I want you to think very carefully before you answer," he said.

"No, sir. She never mentioned that at all."

"You say that sometimes she got there before you did. Do you know at those times if she might *then* have met someone before you arrived?"

"Well, no. I mean, I don't know. But, no, sir. I don't think she ever did that. In fact, when I told her about how remote the place was and that it could be dangerous, she always said there had never been anyone else out there and that the house was probably locked up."

"But you have no way to know for sure that she didn't meet anyone there, do you?"

Jeff said, "Detective Potts, I'm not sure I know what you're getting at."

"I'm getting at the fact that Kerry Blake was wearing this clasp the last time you saw her, which was on Hopper's Lane the day she seems to have disappeared. This clasp proves that either she, or someone else, had this clasp inside the Hopper House that same day."

"Someone else?"

"As far as our records show, you were the last person to have seen her that afternoon. You say you did not go inside the house. You left her on the lane and went home. How did the clasp get in the house?"

"But you said maybe someone else—"

"We are investigating quite a few things that involve the use of couriers for illegal operations. Some of these couriers are turning out to be kids, middle-class, well educated, with no prior criminal record."

Jeff could feel his mouth drop open. "What do you mean?"

Potts said, "I want to know what *you* think."

Jeff was thunderstruck. "You mean—you think *Kerry* might be a *courier*?"

The whole interview had taken a turn Jeff had never even thought of. He said, "No! I mean, look—Kerry is a *nice* girl. I mean really *nice*. And her mother—well, her mother—I just don't think Kerry would be the kind of person to get mixed up in anything like that at all! I *know* she wouldn't!"

The detective was silent, and the silence was awful.

Jeff almost shouted, "And what do you mean by maybe someone else taking that clasp inside that house? That she met somebody and gave it to him?"

"Perhaps she didn't give it to anyone. Perhaps some-one took it."

"What for? And why is Kerry missing? Just tell me that! And why didn't you find her bike?"

"Calm down, kid. Those are angles we need to cover. You happen to be the last person who saw her before she disappeared, and if I'm pumping you hard, it's because I need every scrap of information I can get out of you. Don't you see that?"

Jeff realized he had come halfway out of his chair, and now he sat down again. "I'm sorry," he said.

"I understand how you feel. But I have a job to do. A very difficult job, and I need all the cooperation I can get."

"Yes, sir."

"And you *have* helped, I'll tell you that." Then he paused. "There's only one thing that bothers me, though. About your whole testimony."

"Sir?"

"You repeatedly said that you had been *running* out Hopper's Lane way when I know you are barely coming off a badly broken leg. And the day you had to leave Kerry there on that lane by herself, the last time you saw her, you had to leave because you had a crucial evaluation appointment with the doctors at the orthopedic clinic."

Jeff looked down at his lap. "Well, maybe I did hedge about the leg, and I'm sorry about that, sir. It's just that —well, it didn't have anything to do with Kerry or the Hopper House or anything. I didn't think it was important."

"Everything about this case is important. I will want to know what kind of shoes you wore, just where Kerry sat opposite the house, everything you can show me and tell me about every time you saw her out there. Particularly that last day. Were you wearing different shoes then?"

"Yes, sir."

"We'll need to see those too. If there are other prints there, then that will tell us something about what might have happened after you left. Now do you see how important every last detail is?"

"Yes, sir. I guess I was just trying to tell you everything about Kerry. I didn't think I mattered in it."

"You do matter in it. I'm going to need you all the way through, as far as you can take me. And, incidentally, I'm very glad you got a good report from the doctors on the leg. You're not a bad track man. Maybe you'll get back with it yet."

Jeff looked surprised. "You knew all this all the time?"

"We don't call anyone in here without checking into what kind of answers we think we'll be getting.

"Now I must caution you not to mention any of this to anyone. What you and I have talked about is strictly confidential, and I don't want you discussing anything we've said, or anything at all about Kerry Blake with anyone. That includes your parents, your brother, your friends, and especially reporters. Or, and I emphasize this, any casual acquaintance or stranger at school or otherwise who might ask a few innocent-sounding questions. Is that clear?"

"Yes, sir."

Then Potts stood up, and the interview was over.

It wasn't until later that Jeff remembered that the hand on his arm leading him out of the office had been firm but gentle. And that in the hallway he had been told—not once, but twice—that he had been extremely helpful.

And remembered with a jubilant burst of excitement that Potts had said he'd be calling on him again soon.

But what finally came into focus out of all the chaos, what came with the clarity of a beacon shining into a black hole, was the fact that the form he had filled out weeks ago for the police cadet program was there on Potts's desk. His application had been right there on the desk the whole time, and Potts had said how glad he was the leg was going to be okay.

Jeff wanted to shout with joy. Suddenly he felt ten feet tall and his leg didn't hurt a bit. He had helped them about Kerry. And they at least *knew* about his application.

12

When Sandra Blake answered the doorbell, flashbulbs went off in her face. She started back inside only to have the door held open by two reporters who thrust microphones in her face. She could not see clearly after the explosion of lights, and she jerked at the door, trying to wrest it from the hands that held it fast. She could hear the questions popping loud and fast, like the lights, and her own voice saying, "I have nothing to tell you! Please leave me alone!"

Then Allen Davidson bounded up the steps. He stood between her and the newsmen and gave Sandra a little shove into the apartment. She was too upset to hear what he was saying out there, but in a few minutes she heard cars leaving. Then the doorbell rang again.

"Sandra—it's me, Allen. You can open up now."

And when she opened the door this time, Allen was standing on the stoop juggling two full sacks of groceries.

"I came as soon as I could," he said. "I would have been here sooner, but I was on an official errand for Tony Perez at the Hopper House."

Sandra watched him make his way to the small kitchen, where he set the bags carefully on the side of the sink. He turned to her then and took her hands. She longed to rest her head against him as she had done when he walked into this little apartment for the first time—and, she thought, into her life for real. But today there was something different about him; there was a suppressed excitement in his greeting.

So she said, "Thank you for coming, Allen," and took her hands away. "And thank you for making those reporters leave. I just couldn't take their questions after those awful phone calls last night."

"The phone company has already been here?"

Sandra nodded. "And the police. A very pleasant and efficient young man in plainclothes—a detail, I'm told. They are keeping a round-the-clock watch on the apartment." She tried to sound coolly businesslike, but her voice wouldn't cooperate.

"They've checked you out on how this phone device works? When and how to turn it off for personal calls, all that?"

"Yes. I think I understand."

"But it's not going to be easy for you."

She hoped he would remain businesslike too. Maybe then she wouldn't crack.

He said, "There will undoubtedly be more calls like those last night. And others just as sick. But if a call should come through about Kerry, whoever it is will have to hear your voice in order not to be scared away. Can you handle that?"

"Anything is better than this waiting." She had turned away from him, doing something busy.

Then she felt his hands on her shoulders, turning her around. He looked at her a long minute, and she saw again the deep concern she had seen before in his brown eyes.

"Meet your new in-house officer," he said. "Special Assignment."

"But—"

"But nothing. It's official business for the police."

He was at the sink now. "Meanwhile I've notified my office where I'll be, and I have permission to have any urgent calls relayed here. Just remember to punch the right button. And I've brought enough groceries for lunch, supper, and breakfast. Now what would you like for lunch? A hamburger? Say yes because I'm pretty good at those."

"I won't argue with you. But please let me help. It's better to be busy and not think."

She watched him unload the grocery sacks, and she put the perishables away in the refrigerator. She and Ted used to do this—Saturday was always their big day to shop, and it had been fun together, searching for specials, stretching their budget so that they could afford the things they wanted. This sharing small domestic chores was one of the things she missed the most, and she found herself now frighteningly grateful to Allen for filling this void. But this too was impermanent and fragile, and she knew it.

When the bags were empty, he creased them neatly and handed them to her. "Good garbage bags," he said, and that, too, was like Ted. He had been a natural recycler.

While Sandra set the table Allen patted out the ground beef for hamburgers and cut up a small salad. The meat had just begun to sizzle when the telephone rang. The sudden cold grip of last night's horror returned as Allen nodded to Sandra, indicating that she should answer.

Lifting the receiver, she found it necessary to clear her throat before she could speak, and when she managed, the tightness, the dread mixed with anxiety for word of Kerry made her voice weak.

"Hello," she said, her shaking hand poised near the control button.

Again there was only the sound of breathing, but now she had police instructions, and she started talking.

She said, "I know you're calling because you've heard or read about my missing daughter. I think you are trying to help me find her. Have you seen Kerry? Do you know where she is? Tell me, please . . ."

And with Allen standing close beside her, his hand on her arm, she managed to go on saying the things Chief

Perez had told her would make a person hang on to the line, maybe say something helpful to the case. But no one spoke. She shook her head at Allen. He squeezed her arm, then took the phone from her trembling, wet hand and hung it up.

"Oh, God," she whispered. "Did I do it right?"

"You were perfect. Tony will let us know what they find out. Now I've got to try to call our friend Mrs. Murdoch again."

"Mrs. Murdoch?"

"Yes. I've been trying to get her ever since I left Tony. We need her blueprints of the Hopper House."

Carl had not gone far before he knew the ache in his groin was going to mean trouble: it had begun to swell. Each step became more painful, but he walked on—ever more slowly—until he felt he had to stop. The bridge he remembered crossing the night before was not far ahead. If he could get there, he could go down and soak in the cold water.

The road leading away from the old quarry was even more remote and deserted than it had seemed last night. The fields they had passed, and even driven across in the van, were overgrown and neglected. He had not seen a car all morning. Nothing had passed him coming or going: Ax had not come back yet to look for him. But there was no hope of flagging a ride either.

Once he turned and looked behind him as far as he could see up the empty, twisting road he had covered in the hour or so he had been walking. He didn't know what

he expected to see back there—and there was nothing—
but he sensed that he was not alone. Of course, it could
be the girl. She would be getting out of there, too, and
since he was having to walk so slowly, maybe she was
catching up to him. This was the only road, so what other
way could she go?

Finally he reached the bridge and pushed through the
weeds and brambles and went down to the bank. There
was a cool clamminess in the air under there and it was
dark with shadows. He lay down on the clay-caked
grasses; it was dry on the bank now and he was tired. He
stretched out, his head propped on a log. He would rest a
little while, then wade in the water and hope its coldness
would ease the swelling and ache.

He tried to make his mind a blank, but when he closed
his eyes he saw the scar on Ax's face as it had looked in
the gloom of the basement in the old house in Blanton. I
should have got out then, Carl told himself. It was all
wrong from the beginning, waiting for Benny. But he
knew, even more than that, that he'd been stupid to get
mixed up in it in the first place.

So he hated life in south Georgia. So he hated working
for his dad and uncle. When they had first gone to Jesup,
he had hoped to be just like other kids. In Chicago he'd
been jerked in off the streets because the old bat in the
flat above watched from behind her curtains and told his
parents everything he did. He did plenty she didn't see.
But he never liked the fighting, the ganging up. That was
just how you survived in Chicago.

His parents' whispered conversations had kept him

awake into stuffy nights. Things had got so rough, they were even afraid to leave a window open. Then calls from his uncle who had gone south. The move in the U-Haul. He wasn't very old, but old enough to hate living in the house trailer stuck in a flat of pine woods, hate the way it shook on its concrete blocks when you walked, or just shut a door.

The dreaded first day at the new school. The line-up of guys that circled him at recess, jumped him, shoved him until he beat hell out of the one he knew, at last, was their leader. And that leader became his best friend.

Carl began to grow. It was a joke—Carl, the Battleship, the leader, Dinghy. Carl won that one thing: He outgrew Dinghy and that's how Dinghy got his nickname. But Carl never wanted to be a leader. He wanted a friend.

Then the goddam tree business. All Carl's hopes had gone toward making the high school football team. He was big now, fast, powerful. He had the hands. It would have meant winning his own place—maybe even without Dinghy. But no. His dad and uncle "needed" him to work the tree farm.

More whispered conversations through paper thin walls of the trailer. His mother's voice piercing, even when at a whisper; his dad—such a soft-spoken man—no way he could stand up to her. His mother didn't like the company Carl kept.

Company, hell! Those guys were the first real friends he'd ever had. And no goddam old bat with her eye to the window because they lived so far out in the boondocks there wasn't anyone else except his uncle and aunt down the road in the *real* house his mother wanted so bad she couldn't stand it.

So Carl should work the farm. Right along with Sway and Hutch and Mulehead and Deadman. Only they got paid. He worked. Day in, day out. After school and every weekend. He knew he was a good worker. The Blacks liked him. His dad needed him. Well, goddam it, pay him then, or shove it!

He wanted his own wheels. He wanted some jingle in his pocket, and he damned well wanted his Saturdays the way he wanted them and not the way his mother did.

Oh, cripes. Everything changed. They gave him his Saturdays if he'd go to church every Sunday. So he went back to work. His dad slipped him a few bucks, no real pay. Carl pretended they were "bonuses" instead of handouts and the steady hands let him think they believed that, only he knew they didn't.

He still didn't have his own cycle. He had to wait for Dinghy. The Battleship riding double behind the little guy all the way to Brunswick on Dinghy's Suzuki. What did he have to lose?

Maybe he could have stuck it out for one more year of high school, then gone away to college. His dad had promised him that. Now he knew he had blown his chances, and anger at himself and everyone else became the ache in his gut until he wondered if he could just keep his eyes shut and die.

Everything had gone wrong. Everything possible. And what was he going to do now? He felt drained, absolutely wiped out.

Suddenly he opened his eyes. He listened. Something had moved on the road behind the wall of brambles and he eased the .38 out of his belt and rolled painfully onto his side, waiting and watching. He could see the bushes and tangles of briars twitching. He sat up.

And then the girl was standing there. She didn't seem surprised to see him.

"What do you want?" he demanded.

"I want to know where I am," she answered. She came into the shadow where he was and sat down not far from him. She looked with little interest at the gun in his hand, as if it no longer mattered to her. "Where am I?" she said.

"Tennessee."

She let out a long sigh and brushed the hair out of her eyes.

"Look," Carl said, "just get out of here, will you? I gave you your chance back there at the quarry. Now, goddam it, beat it."

"Just keep walking down this road?" she asked. "I've been walking for miles and haven't seen a sign of civilization. The van made a lot of turns. I have no idea which way to go. I'm afraid I might end up back at that motel."

"Well, just get out of here. I don't want any part of you. I don't want to be responsible."

She looked at the gun with a small, unamused smile. "You think Ax and that man are coming back, don't you? Why else would you be hanging onto that gun like that? Well, do you think I want them to find me either?"

"Beat it," he said. "I mean it."

"No." She didn't get up. She wrapped her arms around

her legs, her chin resting on her knees. She looked at the river, sitting very still.

It was true what she said about Ax and Jerry. He *was* afraid they would come back. Maybe he had hit Jerry when he fired at the windshield. Maybe that was why they hadn't already come. Ax would probably know a doctor to fix Jerry up, just like he knew about the motel and Benny coming to that house in Blanton. Ax would know everything he needed to know to keep alive and get his share. And the first thing he would do to keep himself safe would be to get rid of Carl, because now he really did know too much. And so did the girl.

Everything that had happened swept chaotically through his mind, and he felt sick and overwhelmed by it all. Nothing made any sense anymore—him here under this bridge with this girl sitting there.

Suddenly he remembered the thing Benny had given him while they were standing by the car. Now Carl reached in his pocket and drew out the small piece of cardboard. It was the flap torn from a pack of matches Benny had evidently picked up in Florida, because there was an ad for a bar and grill with a Florida address on it.

Carl turned it over. On the blank side Benny had printed *The Mantle*. Carl looked at the words, puzzled.

"What is it?" she asked.

"I don't know. It's something Benny gave me back there at the quarry. I don't know what it is."

He handed it to her.

" 'The Mantle,' " she read. "Why did he give it to you?"

"I think it was something he didn't want Ax to have.

Maybe it has to do with what he was after in that house in Blanton.

Carl stuffed it back in his pocket. "Jesus, I'm tired," he said.

He looked at the girl. "Go on. Get out of here. I mean, I'm telling you for the last time."

She shook her head and looked away.

"I mean it," he said. "Because—because if you stay with me, you are going to be a hostage. And don't think I wouldn't shoot you if I had to."

"I know that," she said. "It's just that I would rather take a chance with you than—" She swallowed and looked at him. "You think he'll try to find us, don't you? You think Ax will come back."

"I know he will."

"I won't give you any trouble," she said. "I promise. Then when we get to a city or town, you could have time to get away. You could just leave me, and I could go home."

"You make it sound simple. It's not that simple."

"No. I know it isn't, but I don't know what else to do. All the time I was walking back there behind you I kept thinking, what if Ax came back and what if . . . And then I saw you go under this bridge, and I decided I'd be better off with you than alone."

Carl needed time to think. Whatever else he did, he knew he didn't dare stay on this road any longer. He'd figured he should try to follow the river until he came to the railroad spur they'd crossed last night, then maybe head along it.

But what would he do with this girl tagging after him? She was going to follow him, anyway, it seemed, so why not just take her as a hostage and keep her with him? There were only two cartridges left in Benny's .38—not enough to defend himself with. Maybe he could use the girl as bargaining power. Not with Ax—Ax would kill them both if he found them. But with the police, if he got caught. There was no way he could shoot his way out of a situation like that, but maybe he could control the girl with the threat of those two bullets. Maybe, as she said, she wouldn't give him any trouble. Maybe it would work out better all around to keep her with him. And when they got to a town, well, then—then he would figure it out from there later.

"Oh, Jesus," he thought, "what a mess." What did he know about hostages?

"All right," he said. "But from now on you do exactly what I say. And right now you go downriver there and stay until I tell you. I've got to get in the water."

13

Jeff showed Detective Potts exactly where Kerry always sat on the little hump of grass opposite the Hopper House and told him how she always left her bike leaning against the yellow poplar. He had brought the two pairs of shoes Potts had asked for and watched the special team go over the area, taking casts, searching the ground for trace evidence. He had to wait in the car while all this was going on, to keep from trampling the area, and he watched, fascinated, as the men worked. Then having been cleared by his portable radio on use of the driveway, Potts drove Jeff up to the old house.

Now Jeff waited with the detective for Mrs. Bertha

Murdoch to bring the architect's drawings her committee had commissioned for a senior citizens' art center. They waited in the huge front entry as her car came slowly and uncertainly up the slope and crept to a stop.

The house was divided and marked off, inside and out, for the special search team, and Potts made sure that Jeff kept to the one small area allotted to him as the men moved in and out with their equipment. Jeff had not expected to be allowed inside the house at all, and he sure wasn't going to do anything to make Potts wish he'd left him out in the car.

Jeff had never been in such a house before, and he found its enormous emptiness overpowering. He thought of Kerry wandering alone through its echoing rooms and a sick frustration came over him because he had not been able to prevent whatever it was that had happened to her.

He stood beside the detective as they watched Mrs. Murdoch gather a large roll of drawings together from the front seat of her car. She, too, had brought the shoes she had worn the day she was in the house with Mr. Davidson and Kerry's mother.

"I'm so glad Mr. Davidson asked me to come," she said as she limped up the steps. "I didn't want to make a nuisance of myself, but I did think these studies might be helpful to you." She came breathlessly into the entry hall, offering her hand to Potts.

"Mind you stand behind that chalk mark, please," Potts said, and he introduced Jeff.

He thanked her for bringing the shoes, handed them to

one of the technical squad, then spread the drawings on the floor beside the plans the realty company had provided. Jeff squatted down beside him, and in a moment, with knees bending audibly, Mrs. Murdoch joined them.

"I really do hope these are helpful," she said. "The architect couldn't have been more thorough in his evaluation of the house. And in studying the heating system, he found that some of the ducts weren't connected. The worst section is under the kitchen. Apparently over the years as old flooring rotted out new flooring was laid without tearing out the old boards. The ductwork there would all have to be replaced. And he said all the old boards should come out because they will eventually give way. Right now there are large spaces in there. And that's where the ductwork would all have to be redone."

"What do you mean, spaces?" Potts asked. "Are there actual holes under the floor?"

"Yes. He showed me where. You can see it if you get behind the furnace. At least, barely see it. There is a maze of new and old flooring the full length of the kitchen. Fortunately he was a small and wiry man and could crawl all up in there. And he found the ducts were just hanging loose about halfway back."

Potts unclipped a walkie-talkie from his belt and gave an order. Two men reported immediately.

"Let's take a look," Potts said, and he helped Mrs. Murdoch to her feet. "You may go now," he added. "I'll see that these drawings are returned when they can be released. I think these might be helpful to have."

Jeff was amazed at the matter-of-fact tone when he

himself could hardly keep his mouth shut, he was so excited.

For a moment Mrs. Murdoch seemed disappointed to be dismissed. But she said, "Remember, you can't see it unless you're behind the furnace. What looks like the flooring of the room above isn't that at all. There's an opening between it and the other layers of floor."

Potts handed the drawings to one of the men.

"Jeff, you stay behind that chalk mark. You are not to leave that area."

"Yes, sir."

Then Potts headed for the basement with his men.

"Oh, I do hope this is helpful," Mrs. Murdoch said again, earnestly. And then she sighed. "Well, I suppose there is nothing more I can do. Good-bye, Jeff." Another sigh, as she seemed loath to leave. "I suppose they *will* let me know if—well, if all this is helpful." She started toward the door.

"Wait," Jeff called. He saw no reason why he couldn't help her down those steps to her car if they kept within the chalked pathway. He took her arm.

"Why, thank you, Jeff. It is a bit hard going up and down with this gimpy knee."

"I know how that is," Jeff said. "I broke my leg, and it was pretty hard to get around there for a while."

He opened the car door for her and helped her in, then waited while she fumbled with her seat belt before carefully closing it.

She looked out of the window at him intently, as if she were studying him. Then she smiled and reached out her hand.

"You are a thoughtful young man. And kind. Now you'd better get back to your chalk mark before that ferocious detective eats you up."

Jeff laughed and waved her on her slow, cautious, old-lady way down the long curving drive.

By prearranged signal the plainclothesman on duty outside Sandra Blake's apartment called Allen Davidson out for a report. While she waited anxiously Sandra walked restlessly about the small room, realizing in the length of time he was gone what Allen's presence had meant to her.

He had been gone a long time when she went into the kitchen to make tea. The clock on the stove said five; the endless day was settling into the gloom of a fall evening with rain hovering in a heavy sky. The days of waiting were bad enough. But when night started coming down, Sandra's fears for Kerry's safety congealed into such an anguished ache of concern that she did not see how she could get through the next few hours.

When she heard Allen returning, she set the cup shakily on the coffee table and hurried to the door.

He saw the pleading in her eyes and led her to the couch. "No." He shook his head. "No word from Kerry yet. But Potts has found the stash in the Hopper House. Drugs—enough to make him think this is not just a small-time operation."

"What kinds of drugs, Allen?"

"Plenty. Primarily marijuana. Plus heroin, cocaine, hashish, methaqualone. Doggoned clever. Sealed in foil or small instant-coffee jars and put in rough canvas bags to make further prints practically impossible to lift clean. Potts just hopes he hasn't blown his chances at getting the courier that was probably going to take it from there."

"Oh, Allen—"

"At least this gives us an angle," he said. "Now we know the direction a search must take. Because someone obviously knew the layout of that house well enough to have been in on some of its past construction. Now we do a rundown on everyone who has ever done any work there."

He put his hand under her chin and lifted her face so that she was forced to look at him. "It's a beginning, Sandra."

She tried to believe that there would be time—time to find Kerry before it was too late. She bit her lip and nodded.

"I know," Allen said. "I know. Hang in there, sweetheart. Just hang in there. Something's got to break our way soon."

14

Kerry's jeans were wet and torn and covered with burrs.
The scratches on her legs stung. She had been following
Carl for hours down the riverbank, and as he plowed
doggedly ahead through the near-impassable, thick, tangled growth, branches whipped back in her face, and
she was constantly getting entangled in thorny vines. She
dropped a little behind him, but was afraid to let him get
too far ahead for fear he would leave her.

Then Carl stopped. "I think we've got to find a place
to cross over," he said. "The river looks like it's bending
away from the spur line. And besides, the other bank
doesn't look as rough."

She watched him ease down to the water's edge. "It's too deep right here," he called up to her. "But a few yards farther down it looks shallower. Give me a hand."

She hung on to a thick vine, dug her feet in, and reached down to pull him back up the bank. They continued their slow progress to the point Carl had seen and together made it down to the water's edge. Carl took off his shoes and socks, and Kerry followed his example. He rolled his pants up as far as they would go, tied the laces of his shoes together, stuffed his socks inside, and slung them around his neck. Then he began inching out into the water, testing its depth. He cautiously worked his way several paces out, slipping and half-falling on unseen rocks and holes, but the water appeared no deeper than mid-thigh.

"It's cold as hell," he said. "But I think you can make it. When you get this far, grab my hand. It's tricky, so watch out."

The current was swift, dragging them downstream, but somehow, clinging to Carl, Kerry inched her way along. Once she stepped in a hole and nearly slipped all the way under, but he pulled her back up. The water was freezing, and she could barely feel her feet or legs by the time they reached a flat rock on the other side and crawled up on it to rest.

Then they were ready to begin walking again. They walked in silence, exhausted and cold. This side of the river seemed just as overgrown and difficult as the other had been. But Carl was right. The river was bending away from the direction they wanted to go. He led them off at an angle and somehow held a course to a clearing.

When they came at last to the spur line, the walking was easier. They would follow the track until they came to a town. It had seemed logical when Carl had announced the plan, but they had walked most of the day without seeing a trace of civilization, and now it was getting dark.

All around, the mountains humped like a barrier. Walking the track was easier, Kerry supposed, than cutting through those rugged hills, but she longed to find a house, a place with a telephone, with food and a clean bed. They had found apples in an abandoned orchard, sour, wormy apples that puckered Kerry's mouth. She had thought she would never be able to eat until she reached home, but now her stomach was crying for food. Along the river, water had been no problem, and they had sucked up the cool cleanness of fresh springs. But there were no springs near the track. Her clothes had barely begun to dry out, her shoes and socks miserably uncomfortable on her feet.

She had lost all track of the days. Her watch said six o'clock, but how long had it been since Ax had shoved her into the back of the van for the first time?

With the thickening darkness the cold increased. Carl had to stop often now to rest, and when he did Kerry nearly froze. Her legs were weary from trying to walk the old crossties of the ancient, overgrown roadbed that seemed to be carrying them up an endless, hopeless track.

Then in the growing darkness ahead loomed the shape of a boxcar on a siding. Surely that meant some sort of traffic was near! Kerry searched the sky, hoping to see a telltale glow of a city's lights reflected there, but only the coming night hovered over the car, an empty night except for black, threatening storm clouds.

Kerry stood beside Carl, looking at the boxcar, wondering what to do. He had spoken little all day. Now he said, "Wait here. I'll check it out."

She watched him proceed cautiously up the track, saw him hesitate a long minute before he swung himself up inside and out of sight.

Kerry held her breath. Except for the rising wind, the scudding of windblown leaves and grasses, all was quiet. Then he reappeared and leaned out of the opening, signaling her to come on.

She stumbled toward him. He reached out a hand and pulled her up into the car with him.

"It's going to rain," he said. "We might as well stay here. At least we'll be dry."

It was too dark inside the car to see anything distinctly, except that it was empty. She wondered what the car had been used for, or if a train ever really did run along this track. How long had this car just been sitting here?

In the far corner she saw a heap of leaves and she wondered if they had blown in, or if the pile was some animal's nest. She could barely see Carl where he stretched out on the floor, his hands locked under his head. She sat down not far from him and took her shoes off, wriggling her blistered toes and rubbing her feet.

"I wish we had something to eat," Carl said.

She nodded in the darkness. "Me too."

"That goddam Ax!" he blurted. "I should have known it was going to end up like this!"

For a long time he didn't say anything more and she waited. Outside the wind swelled angrily. Lightning split the blackness, illuminating the opening in the side of the car, then flickered—little licking spurts of brightness—as thunder rolled, making the floor vibrate. In the eerie light she thought Carl looked dead, he lay so straight and still.

Kerry said, "Carl?"

Silence.

"Where are you from?"

But he didn't answer. Maybe he was afraid to tell her, to let her know too much about himself.

She went on, "I'm not being nosy, really I'm not. It's just that—Carl, please let's talk to each other. I'm so miserable and afraid."

She heard him shift with a sigh. "Down around Jesup," he said at last. "You probably never heard of it. South Georgia."

"I know where that is!" she cried, delighted. Suddenly Carl seemed like a long-lost friend. "We used to go through it on the way to the beach. On the way to St. Simons."

"Not really *in* Jesup. We lived outside, toward Brunswick. My dad had a business with my uncle. Pulpwood and turpentine. I helped after school and on weekends."

"I bet we drove right by it!" she said.

She could picture him, his tall, muscular frame, his sun-bleached head, working under the hard blue of a south

Georgia sky. She remembered the monotony of the drive along that flat stretch, mile after mile of loblolly and slash-pine groves, nothing else but the straight unrelieved road. And she remembered, too, how that stretch always seemed to depress her father. "This must be one of the most uninteresting regions in the country," he had said. "Not even any real change of season for relief. What do people along here do for mental stimulation?"

"Were you born there?" Kerry asked. "You don't sound like a south Georgian."

"My parents are from the North. I was born in Chicago. They couldn't take the bad winters anymore, so they decided to move south. I was eleven."

"Oh," Kerry said. "That explains it."

"Explains what?"

"The accent—or the fact that you don't have one."

After a minute he said, "Yeah. That might have something to do with it. I mean, why they put me in a van with Ax and the Minnesota tag. Because I don't have much of an accent. I could be from up there. Ax could be too. Most of the tags we had were farther north."

"Carl, what were you doing in the Hopper House in the first place? How did you get in there?"

"The house in Blanton? We had a key."

"But how? Where did you get a key?"

"The guy—the bankroller. He has keys to vacant houses all up and down the country."

"But what did you do in there?"

"We left our stash. The haul we picked up from the shrimp boat near Darien." He was quiet a minute. Then he said almost plaintively, "The other guys were supposed to pick it up at the house next week."

"What kind of stash?"

"Dope. Ax figured it must have had a street value of over a million bucks."

"But what good did it do you to put it in the house? Don't you have to sell it to get the money?"

"Not the way we worked. It was a big operation."

"But who was going to pay you?"

"I don't know his real name. Nobody goes by a real name. Just like Ax is Ax. Period."

She said, "Carl, why did you get messed up in something like that?"

He did not answer. "Maybe he doesn't even know," she thought. She could hear him shift slightly and wondered what in his life could ever have led him to Ax.

Finally he said, "I guess I did the first job for kicks. There were some guys I hung out with in Brunswick. One day there was a new guy came into the place and sort of talked to us. Didn't really say anything then, just sort of hinted at some big, easy money if we were interested. He got Dinghy outside—Dinghy's a real crazy man—and this guy makes him an offer. Dinghy—he's my best friend—old Dinghy said he wouldn't do it unless I could be in on it too. The guy sort of gave me the once over and said it was okay."

Kerry could hear him shift positions again, and she waited.

"He just needed what he called couriers," Carl said. "You know, to move the stuff. Dinghy got his old man to lend him his truck and we went to this warehouse and picked the stuff up and drove it to Jacksonville and left it in an old house. Then we had to meet another guy in a bar outside of town and he paid us."

"But—why wasn't that one time enough? Why did you do this other job?"

He was silent so long she was afraid he wasn't going to say anything more.

Then, "Money," he said. A pause. "Only that goddam Ax screwed it all up. We should never have waited for Benny. Benny wasn't part of our deal."

Kerry's stomach felt more than empty. What Carl was saying made her sick. Sick that things like that went on; sick that people made money selling drugs.

Then she asked, "Are you really like that, Carl?"

"What do you mean?"

"What a waste," she said. She lay down on her back, on the hard, dirty floor of the car.

In a minute it began to rain, huge heavy drops that splattered on the top of the car and spit in the opening at the side. Carl got up and fumbled for a way to close the door, and presently Kerry heard it sliding shut. She could hear him shuffling past her, groping in the darkness. Then she heard him sit down next to her.

"What do you mean, 'a waste'?" he said.

"You. That kind of a way of making money. You're not dumb. You sound like you've been to a decent school. I don't think you're underprivileged or anything like that. Maybe if you were, that would be an excuse."

"What are you talking about?" he shouted, furious.

"What about you? You were trespassing in that old house, weren't you? What do you think—it's okay for you to break a little bitty law, but wrong if I break a big one? Who do you—" But a clap of thunder erased the rest of his words.

Kerry could feel the wind straining against the car. Rain rattled at the door and hammered the roof so that talk was out of the question. Near her Carl's anger was almost palpable. The last thing she needed was for Carl to turn on her.

But was it just as wrong for her to go in that house as it was for Carl to leave drugs there? No, yet "wrong is wrong," her father used to tell her, and now she was all mixed up.

She waited for a lull in the downpour, then she said, "I'm sorry, Carl. I didn't think of it that way."

"Well, just remember that! And don't go so high and mighty with me anymore!"

She could hear him move away from her to the other side of the car.

But Kerry couldn't let it go. She asked, "What about your parents?"

When he didn't answer, she went on. "Don't they know you're gone? Don't they worry when you don't come home and they don't hear from you?"

"I told them I had a job. I'd be on the road a lot."

He sounded morose, distant, defensive, and still angry. Then she heard, through the shifting sounds of rain and thunder, the scrape of his shoes as he came toward her. He stood over her.

"You want to know? You really want to know so goddam much? All right! I'll tell you why I'm in this. Dinghy didn't want to do another job. He knew his old man was already suspicious because of all the miles we put on his truck that night. But when he told the guy in Brunswick he was through, they wouldn't let him go."

"What do you mean?"

"I mean, he goes outside and the tires on his Suzuki are slashed to hell. The next time he goes home somebody jumps him and beats him purple. After that he gets phone calls—threats—and all the time he's scared of his old man finding out. Now do you know? Do you?"

"Oh, Carl," she cried, "do you know what you've done to yourself? For the rest of your life you'll be running. From Ax. From the police. From all those people who know about you and that you're dangerous to, if you stay alive!"

But if he answered, the rain drowned it out.

After a while the storm began to slack up. The wind died almost as abruptly as it had started, but the inside of the boxcar was chilly with stale, cold dampness. Kerry felt so forlorn she was afraid she was going to cry. It would have been better if she and Carl could have gone on talking to each other just to keep the lonely sound of the rain from getting her down. But he had retreated again to the far side of the car.

She shifted about in an effort to get comfortable, balling up to try and warm herself.

After a while she heard Carl stirring.

She sat up abruptly in the darkness. "What's the matter?" she asked.

"I'm just going to check the door. I'm so goddam afraid of Ax I can't sleep. I'm going to put my shoes in the slot to jam the slide so he can't get in. If he finds us. And the goddam scarface *will* find us, you can bet on that!"

— 15 —

Sandra awoke to the smell of freshly brewed coffee. The night had passed uneventfully, the telephone quiet, and except for the last awful hours toward dawn when her dreams were terrible, she had slept surprisingly well.

Now she hurried into her robe. But when she opened her bedroom door, she realized the apartment was empty. The pillows on the couch where Allen had spent the night were neatly back in position, the blanket folded. In the kitchen she found a note propped against the coffeepot:

> *Juice in refridg. Davidson special ham and biscuits in oven. Home to change, then to check at office, then with Tony at headquarters. I'll*

call you from there, but my secretary can find
me if anything comes up. Ben is man on duty
outside—reachable by telephone if you need
him before I get back.

    A

With the note in her hand she sat at the little table and
poured hot coffee into the cup Allen had set out for her.
Maybe it was too early in the morning to sort out her
feelings, but she wondered if she had ever felt so pro-
foundly grateful to anyone in her life.

She would not examine their relationship further.
There would be a time in the future, perhaps, when they
could sit down together and talk about what was growing
between them. For now she would just hold on to the
fact that she was not alone in her vigil. Allen was there.
He would stand by her through this crisis, and when it
was over—well, maybe it would just be all over for them
too.

She set the cup down and stared at his note. No, she
thought. Don't think about that. Let this be enough for
now. All the same in her heart she did think about it.
And she knew what she felt was not just gratitude. She
was no stranger to love, and although she knew there
would never be a way to replace Ted in her life, she
found in Allen many of the enduring qualities that had
enriched her relationship with her husband.

She folded the note and tucked it into the pocket of
her robe.

Carl found the walking less painful today, but he was still
sore. He and Kerry had left the boxcar about an hour

before and were continuing along the railroad track. Except for that siding, the track went on endlessly before them with nothing to break its monotony. The rain had stopped during the night, leaving crystal drops on the ragged grasses and thistles growing between the rails. In the distance, mountains rose in a blaze of color, a motley frame for buff stretches of old fields dotting the forsaken landscape.

Suddenly Kerry stopped and pointed. "Look! There's some smoke—like it's coming from a chimney!"

To the left, over a grove of trees, Carl saw the blue-gray smoke curling in a lazy spiral through the still morning air.

"There's got to be a house over there!" Kerry said.

Carl looked around for other signs of life, but there was no hint that they were any nearer civilization than they had been before.

"We could cut across that ravine," Kerry said. "Carl, it's got to be a house! What else would be out here?"

But he wasn't sure. It was hunting season. It could be smoke from a camp or a blind. It could even be a still. He hadn't got this far in his thinking. Suppose it was a house. Suppose there were people there and a telephone. What would he do? Kerry would want to call her home, but could he trust her not to turn him in?

"Please," she said. "Let's go over and find out. At least there might be something we could eat!"

Carl was consumed with foreboding. He hesitated, not knowing what to do.

Finally he nodded. "All right. We'll at least find out what it is."

They left the track and headed toward the steady column of smoke. Across the ravine and through a glade the way opened on a small field and Carl saw an outbuilding, an old shed with a harness hanging from it. Beyond that was a small orchard and garden and then he saw the house. It was little more than a shack.

"There's a well," Kerry said. "We could at least get a drink of water."

"You wait here," Carl said uncertainly. "We don't know who might be in there."

He left Kerry standing beside the shed and headed toward the sagging porch of the house. When he got to within thirty feet of it, he stopped. A man had appeared suddenly in the doorway, and he was holding a shotgun. He eyed Carl critically.

"What you want?" he asked.

"Hello," Carl began tentatively. "We're lost. That girl back there by the shed and me. Can you tell us the way to the nearest town?"

"How'd you git here?" the man said without moving.

"We came down the track until we saw your smoke."

The man looked Carl up and down. "Tell the girl to come here." He remained in the doorway, the gun at ready.

"Kerry!" Carl called. "Come on up here."

Carl watched her come slowly up the dirt path. She was tense and scared. When she was standing beside him, Carl turned again to the man in the doorway. A rooster crowed somewhere behind the house. Then the man turned his head toward the dim interior of the room behind him.

"What you think, Ma?" he asked.

A thin woman in a white apron materialized beside him and added her uncompromising stare to his.

She said slowly, "I think it's all right."

"Well," the man said, "come on in, then."

Carl hoped he wouldn't notice the bulge under his jacket and shirt where Benny's .38 lay next to his skin. He and Kerry went up the creaking steps onto the porch, and the man held the screen door open for them.

"Don't git much company," he said. "Lost m' dog to a bear trap last week. Used t' let me know when they was strangers about."

"Do you have a telephone?" Kerry asked.

Carl shot her a quick warning glance. For a moment he couldn't even breathe.

"No phone this side o' the ridge," the man said. "Town's a fur piece iffen you goin' by the track. Be quicker you was t' take the road. Nearest town's Carterton, about twelve mile due east."

He gave directions and Carl listened intently. A sizable town and they could walk down the road. "But is it safe?" Carl wondered.

The woman was looking at Kerry. "Hope you wasn't out in that bad blow last night. It like to've clabbered the milk! You been lost and walkin' like that, you might like a bite to eat."

"Oh, please!" Kerry begged. "We haven't even had a drink of water!"

"Pail's fresh full on the porch. A dipper's hangin' on the peg. A wash pan next t' it, you don't mind cold water. Paw, poke up the stove, and I'll warm the corn-bread."

The man hung his gun on a rack over the fireplace, then he poked the stove. When Carl and Kerry returned from the porch, he turned to them, studying them thoughtfully. Carl had seen him looking through the small window at them the whole time they were out there.

"Now," the woman said, "eat a bite." And she stood aside while Carl and Kerry sat at the plank-top table.

The man continued frowning at them, rubbing his chin. Then he said, "Been a man up this a ways. Come up last night. Said he was lookin' fer his daughter that run off with a young man."

Carl felt himself freeze.

"Man about my size," he went on. "Said he drove up from Statesville thinkin' they might be hereabouts."

Carl saw Kerry's fork stop midway to her mouth. The two of them waited for the man to go on.

"Didn't cotton to his looks," he said. "Had a bad scar. Was drivin' a blue car—a Chevy, guess 'twas." He hesitated, holding Carl with his fixed gaze. "Sound like some un you'd be knowin'?"

Carl blinked. "No," he said. "I don't know anybody like that."

"Good," the man said. " 'Cause I didn't cotton to his looks."

"Now, Paw, you let them eat," the woman said.

"Was there anybody with him?" Carl asked.

"Couldn't tell. Parked back aways, an' 'twas dark. But he had t' circle the yard t' turn around, so I seen the car. Tag looked like outa state."

"Which way did he go?"

"Only way he coulda. Back out th' road. Didn't say where he was headin' fer."

The country food that had tasted so good now stuck in Carl's throat. He could no longer swallow. If he and Kerry went on the road to Carterton, would Ax be there?

The man must have read his thoughts. He said, "Now iffen he come up from Statesville, like he says, then maybe he wouldn't be goin' back thataway. The county seat, town of Eagleton, is just this side of the divide before you get to Statesville. You take a left by the fork by the church. Hit's a good piece from here, but I can't leave off my chores or I'd carry y'."

Carl was aware of Kerry's pale face beside him as she stared down at her plate. What if he just left her here with this old man and woman—went off by himself—got out of the whole goddam thing and headed for Canada? Would she give him time before she got to a telephone and called the cops? Maybe if he got her outside and talked to her—told her—asked her to give him a break. What would she say? What would the old couple say? Or do? Would they let him get away with it? Or would the old man head him off, send for the sheriff, and come after him?

The man had said Ax was in a blue Chevy. Of course he wouldn't be driving Jerry's car with the windshield shot out, but Carl wondered if he would be able to recognize the blue Chevy before Ax spotted him. There were all kinds of Chevys and so many of them blue.

What year? What model? What to look for? And *where*?

The woman had been bustling about the stove and now she handed Carl a small sack and a Mason jar of water.

"Somethin' t' hold you till you get t' town. Paw always likes a little somethin' t' peck at on th' road."

"Thanks," Carl said.

The man cocked his eye at Carl, then at Kerry. "Yer mighty young to be runnin' off," he said. "But I think I'd be runnin' from his kind myself."

"Now, Paw," the woman said.

"It's true. I felt the evil presence all the time he was astandin' in ma yard. You younguns just take care."

"Yes, sir," Carl said.

"Ma and me run off ourself. Been forty-three year now, and we'd do it agin. But you just watch out fer him. 'Cause if he's the devil I take him fer, he'll not stop till he finds y'."

Carl thought, "What can I say?" He didn't dare look at Kerry. At least she wasn't opening her mouth to them about his part in the stash. Maybe he had scared her good when he told her he wouldn't hesitate to shoot her if he had to.

But he didn't like the way the old man was looking at him, and he felt he had to say something. "Thanks" was all he could manage. "We'll be careful."

But he felt trapped. Trapped into taking Kerry with him now. There was no way he could leave her here after all the old man had said.

Suddenly he was overwhelmingly tired. Nothing had

gone right. He knew now he had been trapped from the first. He would never be able to collect for this job, and he would never feel safe again. He was marked. It was true what Kerry had said—he'd spend the rest of his life running because of what he had done. And he knew he could only run so far before something caught up with him.

The look in the old man's eyes grated on him. It was as if he knew the whole story—had known it all along and was just testing Carl out. Well, whatever was going to catch up to him wasn't going to happen here. The old man could just make his mind up to that. He would leave with Kerry, just like he came, and the old man and everybody else could go straight to hell.

"We've got to go," Carl said abruptly. He snatched up the old woman's bundle and took hold of Kerry's arm so tight she winced. "And I mean right now."

He held on to her until they were out of the door. He had no idea what the old man thought of him, and he didn't care. He just had to get as far away from there as he could. And fast.

16

As he drove toward Sandra's apartment, Allen practiced several versions of what Tony had told him, and he could find no way to minimize the shock he knew such a message would bring. If only there had been something really positive to start out with—something Sandra could hold on to while he gave her the rest of it—but there was no such news.

Maybe he should just butt out of it now entirely and let Tony tell her himself. The thought had not even completely formed in his mind before he dismissed it. This was his case now as much as Tony's. And there was no way his feelings for Sandra Blake would permit him to stand aside and let her absorb this blow alone.

It was afternoon already, and he knew she must be frantic for some word. He had not called her from headquarters as he had said he would in his note because there had been no time. And this was not something to be said over the telephone.

He turned up her drive and pulled to a stop behind Sandra's car. The agent who had followed him stopped behind him. Allen sat there for only a moment before he took a deep breath and got out.

"Wait here," he told the agent and went up the steps.

She met him as soon as he reached the door, and he knew she had been watching for him from the window. She stood with the door held open, looking incredibly beautiful and vulnerable. He went inside and shut the door.

The only way he could break the news was not to look at her, so he pulled her into his arms. He said, "There is still no word of Kerry, but they think they have found the van."

He could feel the tension grow in her entire body as he continued to hold her close to him.

"Some hunters found it. In the Tennessee mountains above Statesville. Grady Potts is taking Jeff Andrews up there with him to see if they can make a positive ID."

She pulled away from him then, and the look in her eyes made him hurry on. "A bike fitting the description of Kerry's was in it and they have found a possible suspect. The bike is in fine shape except for a flat tire."

He could not say a slashed tire, or that the suspect had

been bludgeoned and shot at close range, or that the van was busted all to hell in front. He could not tell her, either, that an empty billfold was found not far from the body, or that they were dragging the lake at the bottom of the quarry.

But he said, "Your mysterious midnight telephone caller turned out to be a very scared kid who has no idea why he placed the calls. He used a pay phone at a filling station not far from where he lives. The station attendant was suspicious and had been watching him when Tony's men investigated.

"Tony also says they've made progress on the hunt for workmen who might have been in on some of the renovations at the Hopper House. They have a lead on a previous tenant who ordered some of the work done."

And again, he couldn't tell her that the man had a criminal record as long as your arm and was known to be somewhere in South America.

Sandra continued to stare at him until he could no longer stand the pain in her eyes. But when he tried to draw her into his arms again, she pulled away.

"You're not telling me all of it, Allen. Please don't hold anything back from me."

"All right," he said. "Potts needs a piece of Kerry's clothing to take with him. Something she wears a lot, isn't clean—whatever she wore most recently."

Sandra blinked, standing rigid and still, as if she might fall if she moved.

"You wanted all of it," Allen said. "Well, there it is."

"Kerry's clothes?" she asked numbly.

"Tennessee has some of the best tracking dogs around."

"Dogs?"

"Look," Allen said. And he told her everything he knew as briefly and concisely as he could. A footprint like the one at the Hopper House that looked like Kerry's shoe. The trace evidence in and near the pit where she might have been. "That's the whole report up to date, but the pieces are beginning to fall into place."

"But—Kerry? Nothing but the bike?"

"No."

She turned her back to him and stared out of the window. "Do they have any ideas?" she asked.

"They're hooked into the National Crime Information Center—all information that might be needed and all questions they need to ask are fed into that central computer. The FBI has already started investigating the whole thing."

His heart ached for her as she continued to stare out of the window. "But we need the clothes," he said gently.

"Her warm-ups," she answered without turning. "They're still in the basket by the washing machine."

"Good." He got the suit, bagged it, and tied the label on.

Then he stood behind her again. "Sandra, all outstanding warrants are on that computer. All information about individuals who are wanted—for any reason—is there. The delinquent prints are recorded there. It's only a matter of time now."

"Time?" she repeated dully. "Is there enough time?"

But he had no answer to that. He took the clothes out to the agent who was waiting.

When he came back inside, Sandra had not moved. She still stood by the window, as if frozen, and he knew she had watched him hand over Kerry's warm-ups, had seen the package with the tag. And he knew that what he had done seemed callous. Even brutal. So businesslike, so routine. Kerry's soiled warm-ups with her scent on them to be used by tracking dogs somewhere in Tennessee.

He stopped where he was and closed the door slowly behind him.

"Look," he said, "if you think I'm hopeful, maybe even excited, I am. If you think this is all some kind of lark for me, it isn't."

"No. I don't think you are having a lark."

"I want to get your daughter back. That's what we're all trying to do."

"I know."

He moved to the couch. "Then—well, damn it," he said gently, "come here a minute, will you?" He patted the seat beside him on the couch. When she sat down, he took her hand. "I want you to know just exactly what is going on. Just exactly what we have to do. And why."

The excitement Jeff felt when Detective Potts asked him to fly with him to Tennessee had now turned to a sickening ache. As they followed Sheriff Brightwell of Eagle County in the unmarked car that had been furnished them at the little airstrip, as they made the approach up to the abandoned rock quarry where the van had been found, Jeff felt the way he had when his dog was hit by the motorcycle—as if all the nerve endings in his chest had been seared. The area was so remote, so completely desolate that he tried not to think of what Kerry might have gone through.

Like the Hopper House, this area had been squared off for careful search. Potts stopped the car behind a marker. A narrow pathway to the van had been made by stringing two yellow ropes from the small parking site.

"Stay here," Potts told Jeff.

For an endless time Jeff sat in the car while Potts conferred with the sheriff and the other investigators. He could see the place marked off where the body had been and the partially open back of the van.

Then Potts came back to the car. "Okay, Jeff. Just follow right behind me. We're ready for you to take a look. Don't move out of the cordons and, of course, don't touch anything."

Jeff did as he was told. When they got to the van, the sheriff closed the back end and Jeff was positive it was the van he had seen on Hopper's Lane. Then they opened it, so that he could see the bike. Of course they had dusted it for prints and done all the other things Potts had discussed on their flight: crime scene search and physical evidence and how police went about getting everything they could. But Jeff didn't need a lab report to tell him the bike was Kerry's. He looked at the back tire, and again he felt the pain in his chest. There was something obscene about the gaping hole in the tire that contrasted with a sort of innocence about the huge headlight, the reflector tape in the wheels, the saddlebag behind the fleece-covered narrow seat.

Jeff nodded. "It's Kerry's," he said.

He saw then the gear some of the men were hauling up from the water in the bottom of the pit, and he looked with a haunted, unspoken question at Potts.

Potts said, "They've finished dragging. Nothing specific to do with this case came up."

But Jeff knew what he meant was that there were no fresh bodies down there. He said, "What do you do now?"

"I give them Kerry's clothes," Potts answered. "Then we'll ride back to Eagleton, and I'll post my report. We'll stay in the area and wait for the lab findings and see if the dogs can pick up a trail.

"Fortunately Sheriff Brightwell's had good criminal investigation training and knows what he's doing. Nine times out of ten when something happens in a rural area like this, the evidence is trampled, removed, or thrown out before anything can be determined. If it's ever found in the first place. But he knew there was a bolo for the van, and he has a murder on his hands, so he instructed his deputies to leave everything strictly alone until all the investigators got what they needed."

"What's a bolo?"

"'Be on the lookout for.' There was an all-points lookout for Kerry and the van."

"What about the dead man?"

"They'll have everything they find here analyzed and add all this to what they find in the dead man's clothes and the autopsy. And we're lucky. They are going to rush everything they come up with to the information center. It'll all be put on the main computer—and we'll wait."

"And the dogs?"

"They'll bring them up here to start them off. They have the best tracking dogs I've ever seen, and excellent handlers. Everything points now to the fact that Kerry left here on foot. And so we wait."

Jeff swallowed.

"I know it's tough," Potts said. He nodded toward their car. "Come on. We'll ride back to the sheriff's headquarters in Eagleton, and I'll post my report. Then we'll see what kind of grub they have in this part of Tennessee."

"Okay," Jeff said. "Because either I'm sick or I'm hungry."

"I understand the feeling," Potts said and gave Jeff a friendly shove toward the car. "Let's get out of here."

Potts started the car and they followed the gravel road out. Jeff looked back at the van, then at the big man beside him.

"I wonder," he thought, "what it takes to be like Potts —wonder if what it takes is in me."

He wanted to ask a lot of questions about how long it took Potts to learn patience, to learn how to wait.

Because it would be hard, the waiting. Very hard. But he would learn to wait. Just like Potts had to learn it.

Jeff shook his head. "Just don't make me have to wait too long," he thought. And he was surprised that he had said it out loud.

17

Carl seemed in such a hurry to get away from the old people's cabin that he practically dragged Kerry the first hundred yards or so down the dirt road, hurting her arm. When they reached the pavement, he stopped. She saw him look in the direction of Carterton, which the old man had said was the nearest town. Then, apparently deciding against it, he pulled her after him down the road toward Eagleton.

The road was roughly paved, but narrow, steep, and winding. Trees grew close to the banks along the sides, except where the land fell away to a valley below.

They had walked for miles before Kerry realized that

the church the old man had mentioned was much farther than she had thought. All that time Kerry was conscious of a small plane droning in a low circle overhead.

She thought, "They've found the van and my bike. That's a search plane, and they know I'm somewhere in this mountain country! What if I wait for an opening in the trees and then try to signal? Would they see me? But Carl—what would Carl do then?"

She knew Carl was aware of the plane too. He kept looking up toward the sound.

"I know what you're thinking," he said. "But don't try anything. Because that just might not be the kind of plane you want it to be."

"If it's not the Civil Air Patrol, what else would it be?"

"Someone Ax knows. They use that kind of plane hauling stuff up from South America. If Ax found out about the report on you and the van back at that motel, then he probably used the same radio, or whatever he uses, to get help finding us. So just don't try anything."

Kerry stopped walking. "You're just trying to scare me."

Carl stopped too. "Look," he said. "I *heard* about the planes. I *know* what I'm talking about."

Then he turned, listening. "Shut up a minute. I think I hear a car."

It was a car. Kerry heard it too. Carl grabbed her arm and shoved her over the side of the road into the underbrush.

The car came on—slow—slow. Kerry closed her eyes.

"Oh, God, no," she thought. "Not Ax. Please don't let it be Ax!"

She waited. Carl's arm over her smashed her flat against the rough ground under the bushes. Neither of them seemed even to be breathing, but she could feel the pounding of his heart against her side. The sound of the car's engine hung in the road next to them interminably. Then she realized the car was passing on.

Still they didn't move.

Finally Carl let out a long breath. She felt the pressure release slightly where his arm had been holding her down. But he made no move to sit up.

"Did you see the car?" she whispered.

"No."

"Not even the color?"

"No."

"Do you think he—whoever it was—saw us?"

"I don't know. They didn't stop. Unless they stopped up the road."

Carl's heart was still racing, thudding against her side. Then he took his arm away and sat up. She sat up, too, and brushed dirt from her face and sweatshirt.

"It might not have been Ax," Carl said. Then he added, "I almost wish it had been. At least we would know where he was. Now we don't know anything for sure."

"Maybe it *was* Ax," Kerry said. "Maybe he's gone ahead to Eagleton, and when he doesn't find us there— then, well, maybe he'll go someplace else. Then it would be safe for us."

"I wish I knew," Carl said. "Come on. We might as well go."

Kerry's legs were weak as she followed him up to the road again, and she realized how tired she was. Her socks and tennis shoes rubbed her feet in places she had never been aware of before. She walked doggedly on until she could no longer even worry about Ax. Her feet went to a beat that said home, home, home, and that thought was all that sustained her as she forced herself to go on.

When at last they came to the church where the road forked, Kerry was close to tears of exhaustion. It was late. Slanting bars of afternoon light thrust their way through the leaves.

The church was a plain, unpainted structure set in the V of the forks. It was the only building they had seen all day. Behind it was a small graveyard, and Kerry could see some plastic flowers stuck in the ground. She also saw a water pump, and she and Carl drank greedily of the cold well water. They had long ago finished the water the old woman had given them, and Carl had thrown the jar into a ravine. Now she wished he had kept it. They could fill it again.

To the right of the church, unmarked and unpaved, one fork of the road disappeared around a curve; to the left was the road the old man had said led to Eagleton and, Kerry knew, a telephone. She had held that thought before her mile after mile. She could call her mother. She could go home.

Now, without a word, Carl headed toward the right-hand fork.

"Where are you going?" Kerry said. "The old man told us to take the left fork to Eagleton."

"I know he did."

"Then, what's the matter? Why are you going the other way?"

"Because I don't trust him."

"But you don't have a choice!" she cried. "You don't know where in the world that other road goes, or even if it goes anywhere. It's almost five o'clock, Carl. We've got to get to a town before it gets dark."

"And what if Ax is there in Eagleton waiting for us? You in a big hurry for that?"

"If that car had been Ax, he would know by now we aren't in Eagleton, so that's the safest place to go. And that man said if Ax had come up this way looking for us, he probably wouldn't go back over the same territory."

"And what if Ax *told* him to say that? Just so we'd head out this way? Don't think Ax doesn't have it all planned out. We're not going to Eagleton. We're taking this other road."

"We've been walking for days," Kerry said. She could feel her voice begin to shake as tears filled her eyes. "Please! I just want to get to a town and find a way to go home!"

"We're not going to Eagleton," he repeated.

"Then let me go there alone!" she begged. "I promise I'll just telephone my mother and find a way to get home, and I won't even let on I know you exist!"

"No."

Anger rose like a wave inside her, and Kerry could feel it explode on top of her exhaustion and despair. "Well, what are you going to do—just keep walking the rest of your life? Please!" she cried. "Just let me find a way to go home!"

"You're coming with me," he said. "There's bound to be another town this way."

"And *then* just what are you planning to do?" She knew her tone was dangerously close to taunting, but she couldn't help it.

Carl whirled on her. "Look, you!" he bellowed. "Just you shut up! If it wasn't for you, none of this would have happened. Now start *walking!*" And he shoved her, hard.

Stunned, Kerry staggered backward, unable to keep her balance, and sat down in the road. The sun was behind Carl, his face black with shadow. He looked huge and menacing.

Then, unexpectedly, he squatted beside her.

"Look," he said. "Kerry—I didn't mean to do that. But just don't give me any more trouble."

She couldn't speak. For a few minutes they just stared at each other. Now that she could see his eyes, she was struck by the sharp contrast of his boy's face above his powerful man's frame. She could see the conflict as if it were written across his features—a scared kid in a grown-up's body. Suddenly she was filled with great sorrow.

"We'll walk till it gets dark," he said. "Then we'll find a place for the night. There's bound to be another town."

"Oh, Carl," she said sadly, "I don't think it's really going to make any difference *which* town you get to."

He blinked, and she knew she had hurt him. Then he said, "Well, we're not going to Eagleton."

She nodded. "All right. We're not going to Eagleton."

Still he continued to squat there beside her. She saw the flecks of color in his hazel eyes, and the confusion. It was hard to realize that for this concentrated span of time she had been with Carl constantly. To live so closely and never share with another person the real you was sad. The times they could have really talked, they retreated behind argumentative walls. They were two strangers who had stayed together just to survive. She knew survival for her meant Eagleton. But they weren't going to Eagleton. She was going down this unknown road with Carl, and they weren't even friends.

But there was no more anger in his eyes. Beyond the confusion was something else, something she couldn't figure out. It was almost as if he were seeing her for the first time.

He took her hand. His palm was big, hard, and callused, but there was a gentleness in the fingers that closed over hers. Then in a minute he pulled her to her feet, and they started walking again.

The Eagleton Café was not far from the courthouse where Detective Potts made his report. The town itself was fairly small, with only a few rows of streets making up the business district. Nestled as it was between the mountain ridges, it seemed remote, with only the bus station across from the café linking it to the outside world.

Jeff waited in an anteroom of the courthouse while

Potts made his report and conferred with other investigators, in person and by phone. By the time the detective rejoined him, Jeff was so full of questions he thought he would explode. But he knew that to ask them would violate the rules Potts had laid down. As they crossed the street he glanced back at the big clock in the dome of the building and saw that it was already six o'clock. He knew he should be hungry, but he wasn't. The day had been so full of new experiences for him that it seemed at once very early and very late, as if the hours since he left Blanton had held too much. Or too little. They had not found Kerry.

The café was warm and steamy with the smell of country-fried steak and fresh-cooked greens. Jeff and Potts slid into an empty booth halfway back in the narrow room. The place was filling up with customers, and the one girl who was taking orders already looked tired.

"This is official business," Potts said with a nod at Jeff. "So order all you want."

Nothing on the menu really appealed to Jeff, but he decided on the country steak.

When the girl had gone, Potts said, "Sheriff Brightwell's putting me up at his place, although I'll be spending most of my time at his headquarters. I've booked a room for you at the motel. I want you to stay out of trouble and keep quiet about why we're here. Clear?"

Jeff started to say something, but Potts held up his hand. "Uh-uh. Remember, Jeff, please no questions. What I can let you know, I will tell you. Got it?"

"Yes, sir," Jeff said.

The waitress came back with two steaming plates of good country cooking, and Jeff found he was hungry after all. He and Potts ate in silence.

It was when the waitress brought the apple pie that Jeff saw the man. When he came into the café, he stood in the doorway a moment, giving the customers a hard lookover. He must not have seen what he was looking for, because he turned again and went out. But something of him remained behind for Jeff. His ugliness. It was not just the jagged scar on his jaw. It was there in the sinister way he surveyed the people in the café.

Jeff realized then that Potts was eyeing him with a question.

"It's nothing," Jeff said, embarrassed. Potts had his back to the doorway and could not possibly have seen or felt what Jeff had. "Just because a guy comes in and doesn't see a table or booth free, and he goes back out— doesn't mean a thing." Then he added, "Or does it?"

"Eat your pie," Potts said.

And Jeff obeyed.

18

Night was coming down fast, and Carl began to wonder what to do. He knew by the way the road was becoming less a road and more an old byway that the chances of reaching a town before dark were remote. Already there was a chill in the shadows where he and Kerry continued to walk, and he realized they would need some kind of shelter against the increasing cold of full night.

He was so scared and tired he was getting punch-drunk. He kept thinking back to the last time he'd talked to Dinghy. Dinghy had told him to shut up and leave him alone. All Carl had said was "Ding—do you know what you're going to do yet?" and Dinghy, "Shut up! Leave me alone!" Then Carl had said, "I've decided I'd better do this next job. I'm scared not to. I got to meet a guy near Darien—" And Dinghy had screamed at him, "Shut up! Don't tell me about it! I don't want to know what you are going to do!" and Carl, "But why—?" and Dinghy, "Because I don't want to know too much about it!"

Well, maybe ole Ding knew more than he let on, just like Carl. But it sure shook Carl up for crazy man Dinghy to act so scared. Hell, who had had more fun on that first job than Dinghy? Laughing at Carl because he was chicken right from the start.

And now Dinghy's final words echoed endlessly in Carl's tired brain: "I don't want to know where you're going or who you're supposed to meet or what you're going to do! I don't want to know anything about it at all! You do what you think you got to do, and I'll just have to go my own way. So shut up about it and leave me alone!"

All mixed up with thoughts of Dinghy were the urgent thoughts of escape that had pushed Carl all day. For flight and escape. He could not define what it was that made him so sure he did not want to go to Eagleton. But it was there, like a force thick inside him, a trapped sureness he could not shake. Part of this feeling had to do with Kerry. A very large part of it he didn't exactly understand. And he didn't know how to handle it.

When Kerry had chosen to come with him back at the bridge after the rock quarry, she had come of her own free will. But when he dragged her down this road away from Eagleton where she might have found a way to get home, something in their relationship had changed. In some strange way he had begun to feel responsible for her. And he didn't want to be responsible for anybody but himself.

Ever since they left the church, Kerry had been quiet. At first Carl was relieved that she hadn't taunted him because there were no towns in sight. But now it was getting to him, and it was all mixed up with the fact that something between them was different.

They had passed a kudzu-covered shanty a few hundred yards back, and now Carl wondered out loud if they shouldn't go back there for the night.

"Well?" he asked when Kerry shrugged silently.

"It doesn't matter," she said. "Anywhere. Just so I can sit down."

He saw the white weariness of her face and that made him feel worse.

"Let's go back," he said. "Even if Ax comes on this road, I don't think he'd spot that place in the dark."

Carl had never seen such a white face. It scared him. What would he do if she got sick? He went to the side of the road and broke off two twigs and handed her one.

"Here," he said. "Chew on this. I don't know about you, but my mouth feels like a chicken yard."

She took the twig.

"It's sassafras. It tastes like root beer," he said. "Go ahead, it's not poison."

She put the end of the twig in her mouth, her lips pale around it.

"Come on," he said. "Let's go back to the shack."

He turned back and she followed him silently. The empty house was nearly lost in tangled vines so that only the rusted tin roof and rock chimney were visible from the road.

Carl pushed through the stand of sumac in front of the broken porch. He could feel Benny's gun under his shirt. It felt warm and somehow reassuring as he waded through the tall grasses and brambles, then tested the steps of the sagging porch. Kerry hung back in the road.

He pulled out Benny's gun. "I'll check it out," he said.

Inside the house he had to wait while his eyes adjusted to the near darkness. Something scuttled in a corner, but it was only a field mouse.

He took a sharp breath and stuck the gun in his belt.

"It's okay," he called from the door. "Watch the boards on the porch. They're rotten."

Kerry shuffled through the tangled growth to the door, where he was waiting. Then she went past him and sat down on the dirty floor.

"I can't make a fire," Carl said. "The light would be too easy to spot from the road. And besides, these old chimneys aren't safe."

Kerry sat in front of the black hole of the fireplace, her knees drawn up, her cheek resting on her hands. And then Carl realized she was crying. The soft sound of it startled him. It was like—well, all the times she hadn't cried, when he knew it must be choking her, when he knew she must be inwardly crying in the van and at the gravel pit—like all those times burst loose in her now and she could hardly get her breath.

Carl sat down beside her because he didn't know what else to do. He put a hand on her shoulder, half-expecting her to shrug it off, but she didn't. So he slid his arm all the way around her, gripping her shoulder in his hand. She turned her face against him and cried until only a hiccuping sound was left. She stayed with her head like that against him, and he put his other arm around her, too, until she was quiet.

Then he remembered the food the old woman had given them, and he tore the paper bag open and spread it on the floor in front of them. He waited, but Kerry just looked at it. He handed her a piece of corn bread.

"Eat it," he said. "Here. Eat it. Come on."

She lifted her head and ran her sleeve against her cheeks and took the corn bread.

"It's not bad," he said. "Sort of dry, but at least it's something. There's some hunks of sausage too."

He watched her eat. Drafts from the sagging door swept in, and she shivered. Carl got up and tried to shove the door closed, but the vines had become a part of it, and even when he tore them loose, the door was so warped he couldn't make it shut all the way. He went outside and found a rock. Then pushing the door shut as far as it would go, he set the rock behind it, and it held.

The inside of the shanty was almost completely dark now. He could sense, rather than see, where Kerry was sitting on the floor, and he squatted down beside her.

"Are you okay?" he asked.

She didn't answer. He took off his jacket and sat close beside her. He draped the jacket across both of them, so that their backs at least would be covered. It was awkward and the jacket would not stay in place, so he put his arm around her again to hold it over her shoulders.

He could feel the warmth of her closeness and set himself against it. It made her too real. It made her too near, and he didn't want her nearness to do what it was doing to him. In the motel, when she lay shivering on the floor between his bed and Ax's, it had been easy to let the blanket slide from his bed. But now he was warming her with himself, and it was very different. His complete awareness of her merged with the feeling of being responsible for her, and he was confused. He wanted desperately to straighten it all out.

"Kerry——" he began. "Look. I've been thinking. We're bound to come to another town tomorrow. And I'm pretty sure buses run up in these mountain towns." He stopped, not knowing what direction his words would take him. Then he went on. "I've got a cousin making it up in Canada. I could get a job up there and just wait it all out."

Her silence let him hear the sound of his own breathing, and his words hung without sense in the darkness. He hadn't said what he meant to say at all.

"Look," he said, trying again. "I don't have a record now. I never got caught for what I did before, and if I can get away from this——"

"What is it you want me to say, Carl?"

"Look—I've got money——"

"Benny's money."

"Well, yes. But it wasn't doing Benny any good, was it?" He waited, but she said nothing. "Benny would have given it to me, just like that match cover he gave me back there when he knew Ax was going to kill him. He would have given me his money."

"And his gun," she said tonelessly.

"Well, yes."

He waited, but she resumed her silence. This wasn't what he wanted to say either.

"We'll get to another town," he continued. "I know there will be buses. Then you can get one and go home, and I can go on to Canada. But . . ." he paused. "But I have to know if I can trust you. That you won't turn me in."

She sighed. "I don't think you would believe me if I said it."

"Would you turn me in?"

"No. If you get caught, it will be your own fault."

"What do you mean?"

"I mean if you just let me go home, I won't turn you in."

Relief flooded him like a transfusion. "Look," he said eagerly, "we'll start as soon as we can see in the morning. I've got enough money for both of us. You can go home, and I can go to Canada." The sound of it was sweet. He wanted to believe that it would really all work out.

"We're okay here for the night." Oh, Jesus, let it work out. "We'll start out first thing. It's *going* to work out. Everything's going to be okay. For both of us. Just you wait and see."

She sighed. "I'm so tired, Carl."

"Here—lie down. You can put your head on my arm, and I'll put the jacket over us."

He stretched out beside her, and she put her head on his arm, then moved it to his shoulder. The jacket barely fitted over the two of them, but he felt warm next to her. Her hair brushed his cheek. He turned his face toward it, and even tangled the way it was, her hair was very soft. But he tried not to think about that. He was tired, too, and it was a good thing. He didn't want to do anything about how he was feeling. He didn't want anything to happen to this girl.

He had never felt that way about a girl before. He had always had what he thought of as plastic feelings when he was with the girls he had known. He felt fake, full of bravado, trying to match what his father called smart-ass talk with smart-ass talk, and doing what his mother called going-to-hell kinds of things.

"Carl, if you get on that motorcycle with Dinghy and ride into Brunswick to see those girls, you are going right straight to hell!" And his father, "Let him go, Betty. You can't keep him in a bubble."

And his mother, "Why did we move from Chicago if it wasn't to get him away from the trash that was taking over our neighborhood?"

"He's just glandular, Betty. All kids his age go through that."

"I don't want him going out with those tramps!"

"Come on, Betty—you don't know they're tramps. They're probably—"

"That piece of brass Dinghy brought over here on the back of his motorcycle was nothing *but* a tramp. And you put one glandular kid with one tramp of a girl, and you've got trouble!"

His father's gentle voice. "It's not the tramps that get in trouble, Betty."

His mother, seeming to shrink, lines around her mouth like they'd been cut in with a razor blade. "All right, Jake. You've made your point."

"Look," his father said. "I'll make him put in extra time cutting trees. It'll help him work it off."

"Well, just see he cuts an acre before he goes to Brunswick. Because he's going straight to hell."

And now he *was* in hell. But it wasn't the girls that had put him there. It was that guy that came into their hangout in Brunswick. And Ax. And maybe Dinghy. And maybe even himself.

He pressed his cheek against Kerry's hair for comfort. But she was already asleep.

19

Allen Davidson felt completely let down and inadequate. But what else could Sandra say? Maybe she thought he was taking advantage of the situation, an advantage he would not have if he weren't a personal friend of the chief of police and special-assignments member of the force. He had assumed he would be sleeping on her couch again, that she would want him on duty there until all of this was over.

But Sandra said, "Allen, I'll be all right. The surveillance team outside makes me feel quite secure. And you've done more than enough."

A gentle rejection, but rejection it was. Even Tony

thought the immediate need for his presence at her apartment was not vital at this point.

"So face it," he told himself. "Stay out of her hair. When and if she needs you again—when she wants you —she'll let you know. And Tony will put you back when he thinks it's necessary too."

His telephone was ringing when he walked through his door. He turned on the light and hurried to pick up the receiver, hoping it was Sandra calling him back. But it was Mrs. Bertha Murdoch.

"I hope this isn't an inconvenient time to talk," she began, "but I've been trying to reach you. Mrs. Conway, from the realty company that handles the Hopper House, called to say that the final legal entanglements are resolved, and the house is free. It can now be purchased. I'm trying to set up a meeting with my committee to make our final plans, and since you've been so interested and helpful, I wonder if you will join us? At your convenience, of course. That's why I'm calling you first."

The farthest thing from his mind at this point was Mrs. Murdoch's plans for the Hopper House. He tried to mask his annoyance. "Mrs. Murdoch, I'm afraid my position on the use of the house has not changed. I think it would make an ideal center for all ages in the community, and that is the only way I will introduce it to the council as a whole."

"Yes, I understand," she said. "And that is just what I wanted to say. That I've been thinking about it a great deal. About your proposals and the young people being a part of it. And I thought if you could present it to my committee as you have to me, they might come around too."

"If that's understood, I'll be happy to meet with you."

"Oh, thank you." Then she added, "I suppose there's no further news of the Blake child?"

"No. She is still missing."

"Oh, dear heaven. I had so hoped . . . But you did hear that our architect's drawings played a vital part in finding the drugs in the house? I'm so glad you asked me to let the police use them."

"They were invaluable. Thanks for your cooperation."

When Allen hung up, he stayed by the telephone several minutes before he got up, took off his coat and hung it over the back of a chair. Then he went to the kitchen and made himself a drink.

It was still early evening, and he knew it was going to be a long one. He took his drink to his favorite chair, sat down, loosened his tie, and unbuttoned the top of his shirt. And there he thought over the whole situation. About Kerry Blake and her mother.

After all, the child whose disappearance had brought him and Sandra together did not even know he existed. Sandra was right to put up a stop sign in front of him. Her first concern was Kerry. And when Kerry was safe, Allen would have to start from the beginning in their relationship. He would have to come into it with Kerry strictly in mind. This is what Sandra was trying to make him understand, trying without saying it in so many words. And he knew she was right.

After supper Potts left Jeff on his own, and Jeff wandered aimlessly down the dead street of the little town toward the motel. He stopped. The prospect of the long evening ahead, holed up with nothing to do made him wonder where he might find a newspaper. Anything. He had seen the motel as they came into town, and it looked as dead as the town. He bet there wasn't even a TV in his room, and if there was one, a couple of fuzzy channels of junk.

He looked up and down the street. Didn't this hick town have a movie theater? Everything looked closed up for the night, except the bus station back across from the café. The lone pharmacy he'd passed was nothing but another darkened storefront, and Jeff had to laugh at the old fading gold lettering that read *Drugs and Sundries.* He would have settled for a "Sundry," whatever that was. Just a few doors beyond was the bus station, so he headed there. Maybe it had a news rack, or some paperbacks.

The station was empty except for the balding, horse-faced agent or janitor or whoever was sweeping up between the stiff, uncomfortable-looking benches. No books, no magazines, nothing. For lack of anything better to do, Jeff took a bus schedule from the rack near the counter and sat down on one of the benches to look at it.

"What's a Leaf Special?" he asked.

"Tour bus," the agent said. "They come up this time of year to see the fall colors. You can't go by those times listed there, though. It changes with demand and where they originate from."

"What about these other two?"

"The earliest bus in the morning goes north at eight thirty. The first one south leaves at ten."

"You get much traffic? Many passengers up here?"

"Depends."

"You've got two going through—just those two morning ones?"

"Yep. Until they tell us otherwise."

"How about tonight? You stay open anyway?"

"Yep."

"Well," Jeff thought, "this isn't the most interesting guy I've ever talked to."

The door of the station squeaked open. Jeff glanced from the schedule over at the small man who had just come in. It was the man with the scar. For a minute the man stared at Jeff; then he went over to the ticket agent.

His voice was soft as he asked, "Any news?"

To Jeff's surprise, the agent inclined his head in Jeff's direction. Again the man with the scar stared at him.

"No," he said in that eerie voice. "About his age, but much bigger. Six-three or four. About two twenty pounds. Blond."

"Ain't seen him," the agent said.

"I'll check back with you in the morning."

"Won't be here. Got tomorrow off."

"Well, give your replacement my message," the man said. The soft voice held a command.

The agent seemed unimpressed. He leaned against his broom. "Better give it yourself. Won't have a chance to talk to him."

The small man stared hard at the agent, who went back to his sweeping. He turned again toward Jeff, and Jeff lowered his eyes to the schedule. He heard the man leave.

Suddenly Jeff felt stifled; he wanted to get out of there into the fresh air. He tucked the schedule in his jacket pocket and hurried through the door. There he saw the man with the scar pulling away from the curb in a blue Chevy. A blast of chill hit Jeff; whether a real frost hung in the air or not, he wasn't sure, but he zipped his jacket shut. Why did that ugly little man make his flesh crawl?

The small motel was at the end of the block of the main thoroughfare and Jeff headed toward it, his hands deep in his pockets. Something about the crisp cold made him feel empty; he tried not to think about Kerry, where she might be, or even about the dogs tracking her out there in those mountains. If only he could turn off his imagination. Maybe he should check into that motel and turn on the fuzzy TV.

He signed in with the night clerk, a sleepy fat woman who handed him the key to 109. Scratch TV. Scratch fuzzy. What seemed to be the motel's only set languished in the small office with a handmade sign on it: OUT OF ORDER.

He went outside to look for his room. The ice dispenser and vending machines sat in a recessed area just outside the office, and Jeff saw a man there with a picnic chest in his hand. The man turned, and Jeff saw him clearly by the light over the machines. It was the man with the scar.

Jeff stopped in his tracks, waiting to see what the man would do next. He saw him load his cooler with ice, buy several items from the vending machines, then move out to the blue Chevy parked at the curb. Jeff hurried on to his room.

When he got to his door, he looked back at the blue car. The man was standing there with the door open, staring back at Jeff. Finally he put his cooler and the other things inside, slid in, and shut the door. But he did not start the engine.

The key in Jeff's hand shook as he unlocked the door to 109. He shut the door and fastened the safety chain. It was very quiet. When he heard the sound of a car starting up, he went to the window, looked through a crack in the curtain, and saw the blue Chevy pull away.

For a minute Jeff didn't know what to do. He had the same crazy-all-over kind of feeling about that man that he had had about the dark green van on Hopper's Lane.

"Look," he told himself. "You are overreacting. This is definitely unprofessional and some kind of dumb hunch. So don't be such a lame-brain." But why were his hands shaking?

He called Detective Potts.

For a minute Potts didn't say anything. Then Jeff realized he was writing down what he was telling him.

"All right," Potts said. "Just hang loose, Jeff. And don't you leave the motel unless you hear from me."

20

Kerry and Carl left the shack at daybreak. She walked beside him as if there were nothing else to do, no longer feeling individual blisters on her feet. Scratches and soreness blended together with the total aching tiredness. But today seemed different. She and Carl were friends.

Suddenly Carl stopped. "We're coming to a town."

It was true. The strip of road they had been following since the sun came up seemed all at once to take on importance, as if it really were going somewhere after all. The thick clumps of crimson sourwood and oak, the golden poplars and chestnut oaks now dropped away to open vistas of farmland. The heavy kudzu that had claimed much of what they had passed since leaving the church yesterday was brown here and shriveled, as if someone had hacked it back to make way for the sight ahead. There was a town!

Carl said, "I guess we might as well get this over with now. I don't want anyone to see me flashing this around." He reached in his pocket and brought out a roll of bills. He peeled off seven tens and gave them to Kerry.

Kerry looked down at the money in her hand, and suddenly the sweat-drenched face of Benny rose before her. She had to close her eyes tight to blot out the memory of him back in the motel, sitting in front of Ax like a fat Buddha, his face gray with unspoken pleading because he knew Ax was going to kill him.

She opened her eyes and she and Carl stared silently at each other.

Then Carl said, "Yes, it's Benny's money. But that's the only way we're going to ·get out of here. Do you understand? Kerry—please—"

She swallowed and nodded.

Then he handed her the piece of matchbook cover with the words *The Mantle* printed on it. She took it, then looked up at Carl again. It was as if he were unloading everything—getting rid of everything that had happened to him.

He said, "What time is it?"

"Just after seven."

"Kerry—before we go any farther, I need to tell you some things. Some things that I overheard. In case I don't make it—"

She opened her mouth to say something, but he hurried on.

"It's only if I don't make it," he said. "Remember, you promised not to turn me in if I let you go home."

"What kind of things?"

"About this deal I got myself into. I don't know a whole lot, but maybe—if Ax gets me—" He stopped, then he said, "I had to meet Ax, just like I told you, near Darien. I was standing on this old dock and there were two shrimp boats tied up there. I was supposed to wait there for my new partner. It was Ax, only I didn't know it. I didn't know anything about him, or what was going on.

"Well, I heard these guys on one of the boats talking. They didn't know I was there. They talked about some planes—modified planes that were coming up from South America with drug hauls. And they said something about ag shipments. From what they said, I think they meant trucks with vegetables. Anyway, they hid dope in these trucks and got them by the customs inspectors.

"Then they talked about somebody in Miami and somebody in Macon and Savannah, and somebody in St. Louis. And I heard them say the name Ward—like he was pretty big in the outfit, because these guys talked like he was some kind of boss. And about somebody else big who could launder the money, but I didn't get his name. A banker. Can you remember all this?"

"Carl—please don't talk like that! Ax won't get you—"

"Just tell me if you can remember all that."

"Yes."

He looked around frantically. "I wish I knew where the hell we are."

"There's a man down the road a way. Down there." Kerry pointed. "By that fence. Ask him."

She could hear Carl suck in a sharp, surprised, uncertain breath. She knew what he was wondering.

She said, "Carl, I give you my word. I won't say anything."

He stood there a long time, his face white. Then he said, "All right."

Together they walked toward the edge of the field where the man was tying up wire. Carl stopped abruptly, a safe distance away.

He called, "Can you tell me what town this is?"

The man straightened. "Eagleton," he called back.

Kerry heard the sound in Carl's throat as if he had choked. "But it can't be!" he said.

"It's Eagleton," the man repeated.

"But I thought Eagleton was the other way!" Carl protested.

"You come up the old back road," the man answered. "But you're in Eagleton all the same."

Kerry waited, but Carl seemed too stunned to say anything more. "Ask him about the buses," she said.

"Do buses run through here?" Carl called at last.

"Not like they used to, but they're starting to bring them back. Bus station's on Broad Street. Just keep goin' straight until you see the courthouse. That's Broad. Station's at the corner across from the café."

Carl let out a long breath. His face was chalky now and damp. "This is exactly how Ax planned it! He knew when that old mountaineer told us he had come up from Eagleton way we'd think Ax wouldn't be going back this way. He knew the old man would tell us that!"

"It doesn't make any difference now," Kerry said. "Come on."

"We've been walking in a goddam circle," Carl said. "I just hope we get out of here alive."

"Come on," Kerry said again.

"What time did you say it is?"

"It's seven thirty." She looked at her watch again and shook it. "It may be slow or something, but that's what it says, and it hasn't stopped running."

"We'll head for the bus station." Carl's voice caught again in his throat. "I'll find out when the first one leaves going north. When I'm safely on it and on my way, you can take the first one that goes south. Hell, I don't know —I just don't want anyone to see us in case we have to wait. He said there's a café across the street from the station. Maybe we can wait there."

The blond hair was sticking to his forehead now, but he didn't move. Instead, he put a hand on her arm. "Kerry—please, don't give me any trouble."

"I promised you, Carl. I won't turn you in."

"You give me your word?"

"Yes. I swear."

"Oh, Jesus," he said. Then, "Let's go."

The shrill ring of the telephone brought Jeff up from a deep sleep. It was Detective Potts.

"Come by the courthouse before you do anything else," he said. "I need to brief you."

Then he rang off before Jeff could ask any questions.

Jeff looked at his watch. It was already after seven, and the dim morning light showed accusingly at the edges of the drawn curtains in the small motel room. He dressed as quickly as he could and opened his door. The maid had begun cleaning the room next to his and he could hear the vacuum humming. He had no idea he would sleep so soundly or so long. He had planned to get up early, but now he wouldn't even have time to eat breakfast before he talked to Potts.

He stopped at the vending machines and bought two candy bars and a carton of milk. Only a few cars were in the little parking area of the motel. He saw no blue Chevy.

Hurrying toward the courthouse, he blinked awake to the fact that he was in Eagleton, Tennessee, a long way from Blanton, Georgia. As he walked, shafts of early sunshine dimmed his still sleepy eyes. He knew, in spite of the rules Potts had made, he would have to ask if the dogs had picked up a trail on Kerry. Kerry, out there somewhere in those mountains, far away and lonely in their blankets of fog. But something in Potts's voice had already told Jeff that they had not found her.

Potts was waiting for him on the steps of the building and led him to an office inside. Sheriff Brightwell had made way for a table for Potts to use, and now the detective motioned Jeff to sit down next to him. Jeff recognized the black leather case Potts had brought on the plane; various folders were spread out on the table.

Now Potts slid two sets of drawings in front of Jeff. "Look carefully at these," he said. The sketches showed the van, drawn from different angles, as Jeff had described seeing it late that afternoon on Hopper's Lane. They were identical except for the vague figures of the two male occupants of the cab.

"Do these sketches bring anything back to you, Jeff?"

Jeff studied them, then looked up at the detective. Suppressed hope marked the weary face of the man who had probably not slept at all last night.

"Not just exactly," Jeff answered. "But this bunch is more like what I saw."

"Look at them again. You said you had the impression that one of the men was smaller than the other. In other words, one was a small man, one a bigger man."

"Yes," Jeff said. "But I don't remember thinking the big man was fat. It was more like—well, taller. I'm sure he wasn't fat like this."

Potts leaned back in his chair and rubbed his hand across his eyes. Then he shoved a mug shot over for Jeff to see.

"Does anything about this man look at all familiar?"

"No." Then Jeff asked, "Is this the fat one in the sketches?"

"Yes. This is the dead man they found beside the van at the quarry. But you don't think the bigger figure was fat like this?"

"I honestly don't. This guy looks older and out of shape. The one I could see—well, not really see, but his outline—was like he was maybe young. And well built. The little man was driving."

Potts gathered the papers back together and put them in a folder. He said, "It's only fair to tell you they have not found Kerry. The dogs had a good trail, but lost it at a river not too far from the old quarry. Sheriff Brightwell has ordered a helicopter to scan the river—both ways. It's possible she was picked up by a boat. We don't think she could have made it across the river alone. And we don't think she would have gone that way by herself. It's dense as a jungle, and the going is slow. They're working the dogs along both sides of the river, just in case. But it will take them awhile to work the area to any point she might possibly have crossed over, or been put out of a boat. And," he added, "it rained like hell. We've probably lost a lot of valuable footprints."

"Can I ask you about the fat guy?"

"The prints they got at autopsy identify him as Benny Hudson, also known as Benny Hutchins. Jewel thief. He was employed as a plumber by an outfit that operated out of Atlanta back in the late 50's and early 60's and did some work on the Hopper House. Served time on several counts and was in prison at the time of a big uprising when a couple of inmates were killed and maimed. Trace elements in his clothes match what was found in the sweepings from the back of the van. His prints are all over the steering wheel, too, and that is absolutely all I'm going to say, so no more questions."

Potts rubbed his eyes again. "What time is it?" He swiveled to look at the wall clock. "Have you had any breakfast?"

"I got some stuff at the motel."

"Well, I want you to go back to the motel and stay there until you hear from me. When they can turn their plane loose, I'll let you go home."

Jeff stood up. He said, "Do I have to go home—before it's finished and they find her?"

"Look, son, no one knows how long this is going to take. I don't want to have to worry about you too."

Jeff shifted feet. "Is it okay if I go see if the drugstore is open so I can get something to read? There isn't even a TV that works in that motel."

"All right," Potts said. "But no hanging around and don't go anywhere else. I want you back in that room so I can keep my mind on my business."

Jeff shifted again uneasily in front of the table as Potts eyed him impatiently.

"Sir," he began, "please let me stay until you find her. I promise to stay out of the way. It's just—well, it's just important to me."

Potts looked down at his papers.

Jeff went on, "You don't even have a good picture of her, sir. You haven't ever even really seen her. I mean in person. Nobody up here knows what she really looks like but me. Don't you think that might be—well, might be important?"

"We have six pictures of her, Jeff," Potts said without looking up.

"But they are all lousy! Not a one of them looks like Kerry. I mean really looks like *her*! They're all prissy dress-up shots or posed or fuzzed-out newspaper stuff, and you can't tell what she looks like. I mean it."

The detective sighed heavily. "Well, it is with great reluctance that I admit you are right. But do you know what you are implying?"

"Sir?"

"That we would need you to identify her body. Her dead body. If Kerry is alive and can still speak, she will let us know who she is."

Jeff could feel his face go white.

Potts went on, "I did not want to involve you in anything like that."

"I—I want to be involved, sir. I want to help any way I can. You'd have to fly somebody else up here to do it if I didn't. And maybe she wouldn't be dead, but just not able to speak. You'd have to have somebody who knew her, really knew her, to make an identification, wouldn't you?"

"Yes." Potts got up. "All right. Stay. But I want you out of the way and out of trouble. Is that clear? Go get your magazine and get back to the motel." He stopped Jeff with a hand on his arm. "And if by any remote chance you do happen to spot Kerry before we do, do not—repeat *not*—try to make any contact with her at all. Because she may be with someone you would not recognize as being dangerous. And I don't mean just dangerous to you. I mean to Kerry. If anyone finds out that she has been recognized, they could blow her apart.

If you *should* see her, I want to know it. *But you are to stay clear.* Is that understood?"

"Yes, sir."

"Now beat it, please."

Jeff knew not to push him any further. He headed out to the street.

21

The northbound bus stood ready in the alleyway between the bus station and the chain link fence that separated the loading zone from the street corner. Already passengers that had got off to stretch and use the rest rooms were moving back to their seats. Kerry stood with Carl beside the panting monster, waiting for everyone to be seated and the driver to swing aboard.

Carl had his ticket in his hand, and he stood uncertainly beside the door looking at Kerry. She knew that suddenly for both of them the moment was unbelievable. They had been living for just this escape. But it was also a parting, and now neither of them was ready.

"Well," Carl said. "I guess this is so long."

Kerry's eyes smarted, and she pretended it was the exhaust fumes. She wanted to smile encouragement at him, but couldn't. She said instead, "Good-bye, Carl. Good luck."

"Yeah," he answered. "You too."

She could see the confusion again in his eyes, the same confusion she had seen when he squatted beside her in the road by the church. That seemed a long time ago, and yet the two moments were related. She knew that at those times Carl was truly seeing her and that it was hurting him.

"I don't suppose you'd come with me," he said.

She shook her head.

His face was pale and strained and suddenly, impulsively, Kerry kissed him.

"Take care, Carl," she said.

"What are you going to do?"

"I'm going to the café and get breakfast and wait for my bus."

"Kerry," he said, "I had no idea everything would turn out like this—"

"Neither did I," she said. Then she tried the smile again. "But here we are."

"I just wish you didn't have to wait so long for your bus."

The driver brushed past them and slid into his seat. He looked out at them, his hand on the door handle. "Aboard," he said.

"You better get on, Carl."

She watched him heave up the steps. He took the window seat behind the driver and the door hissed shut. Kerry could see him leaning across the aisle to wave at her, a small, shy, almost childlike gesture, and then as if he were embarrassed by it, he gave her a thumbs up.

What would have happened, she wondered, if she had met Carl some other way? At school, maybe—any way but this. She could still see him there with his thumb turned up, and she shot hers up in return. He waved again, then leaned back in his seat so that she couldn't see his face anymore.

There was nothing left to do now. In a few minutes the bus would take Carl away—to Canada. And maybe there he *could* start over.

As she went back through the small, empty station to the front door, an old clock somewhere struck the half-hour—a lonely, hollow, ancient sound. She stopped a minute and wiped her eyes on her sleeve, then pushed through into the street.

Jeff saw Kerry the moment she opened the station door. He stood frozen where he was in the doorway of the drugstore, the book he had just bought completely forgotten and nearly dropping from his startled hand. From there he could see her cross the street to the café. But he saw something else too. The blue Chevy coming up the street.

He didn't wait to see what the Chevy was going to do. With his heart pounding he turned and started racing back to the courthouse.

The ache in Carl's throat was choking him. From his window seat he watched Kerry until the café door closed behind her. Kerry was gone out of his life forever, and something raw and sore tore at his insides.

In front of him the driver checked the passengers in the rearview mirror and made notes in his log. The huge bus vibrated impatiently, and Carl pressed against the window to feel the cool glass on his cheek. "Jesus," he thought, "why don't we go!"

Then the street Kerry had just crossed was no longer empty. He saw a blue Chevy pull up to the curb in front of the bus station. For one frozen moment Carl stared at it. The image of the blue car seemed to explode before his eyes until his mind held nothing but the car and the small man who was getting out of it.

Ax!

Carl felt the muscles of his stomach contract, and he thought he was going to be sick. He watched, transfixed, as Ax got out of the car and closed the door. Then Carl saw him head toward the entrance of the bus station.

As if a paralysis had lifted, Carl leaned over, his head down by his knees, his only hope that the driver wouldn't try to talk to him, or notice anything funny. What if Ax already knew he was on this bus? What if Ax bought a ticket—what if he got on too?

The blood in the veins of Carl's neck pounded, choking him. His head and eyes throbbed.

"Oh, Jesus!" he cried silently. "Let's go!"

Still bent over, Carl worked his jacket off and, holding

it in front of his face, raised himself just enough to peer over the ledge of the window. He saw Ax, back in the street again. But he was heading for the café.

Kerry was in that café—alone.

The bus began to move. It lurched slowly, drunkenly, over a broken place in the pavement, then turned into the street. Carl could feel the sweat on his face, his hands, his whole body. He could barely breathe for the tightness in his chest, the ache in his throat.

He closed his eyes, squinched them shut, but still he saw Kerry.

"Oh, Jesus!" he whispered. *"That goddamned Ax!"*

In the café Kerry smelled the food, but food was not important to her now. She took out one of the bills—Benny's money—and got change for the telephone. She would call the police, tell them who she was, ask them to come and get her and take her home. She would not wait here in Eagleton until the southbound bus left. Carl was gone now, and she needed protection.

With the change cold in her hand, she went to the pay phone on the wall. It would be hard to keep the cashier from overhearing her, but that didn't matter. The police would come, and the girl would know anyway.

Kerry's hand shook as she found the Eagleton Police listed with the emergency numbers on the cover of the slim phone book. The book hung on a chain and she tried to hold her eye steady on the number, too frightened to remember it for certain.

She lifted the receiver and managed to get a coin into

her shaking fingers. She lifted it toward the slot.

Then a hand came into her view, a small man's hand, thin fingers, black hairs on them, rigid veins sticking up like bas-relief rivers. The fingers were on the receiver hook, pushing it down.

"Don't move," a soft, familiar voice said next to her ear.

Her mouth opened for the scream that had started up from her insides. But as in a nightmare, no sound would come. She felt the hard jab of a gun in her side and heard the soft voice, softer now, so that the cashier couldn't possibly hear it.

"Don't make any noise. Where's Carl?"

Kerry shook her head.

"I want you to listen very carefully," Ax said. "I want you to act just like you are leaving. My car is across the street. If anyone asks, you are my daughter, and I'm taking you home. Now come with me, and don't try anything. If you make one sound, you will be dead."

Jeff was running, running as he had never run in his life. He tripped over a crumbling curb, staggered, nearly fell, then caught his balance, pounding the sidewalk as he raced to the courthouse.

The courthouse and Potts seemed somewhere at the end of the earth. He hadn't realized the few blocks separating them from the bus station were so long. He felt as if he were running under water with a tide moving against him so that he barely moved forward. But he ran on.

His leg really hurt now where he had come down on it unevenly when he stumbled. But it didn't matter. Nothing mattered but getting to Potts.

Ax's grip on her arm was so tight that Kerry's fingers were numb. They were outside the café now. She could see the rear of the bus, a block up the street, on its way north. "Oh, Carl," she cried. Her knees threatened to buckle, but Ax dragged her down the steps to the street. She could see the blue Chevy in front of the bus station.

"If he gets me in that car and drives away with me—" She couldn't even finish the thought.

His grip tightened. "Don't make one sound," the soft voice purred next to her. "Or I'll blow your head off."

And now they were across the street. The blue car swam, rising and retreating before Kerry's eyes, as if she were going under anesthesia. Ax was opening the door. He held Kerry close beside him, the door open.

He was staring at her, his dragging eye, the scar, all fixed on her. "You will get in. I will walk in front of the car. But I won't take my eyes off you. One move, one sound, and you're dead. Is that clear?"

Kerry nodded, unable to speak, unable to take her eyes from his, but unable to get into that car either. She stood paralyzed where she was.

Ax rounded the front of the car. He had put the gun in his coat pocket, but she knew his hand was still on it.

"I told you to get in," he said. He was staring at her across the top of the blue car now, and Kerry felt the whole street begin to swirl.

But there was something else too. So sudden, too sudden to sort out or take in. An arm, a dull sheen of metal in a hand as someone sprang up from behind Ax, a gun pressed against Ax's face. A blond head and she heard a shout, "Don't move, Ax!"

Kerry's mouth was open with the unformed sound of his name: *Carl!*

"Put your hands on your head!" Carl shouted. "Don't try anything, Ax. Get in, leave the door open, and put your hands on your head!"

An awful moment of utter quiet followed. Ax did not move. Kerry could see the dent where Carl pressed Benny's .38 deeper into the flesh of Ax's jaw.

"Get in!" Carl roared. "And if you try anything, I'll blow the rest of your goddam face off!"

Ax slid slowly onto the front seat, his hands on his head. Carl slid in beside him.

"Kerry," Carl said, his voice choked, "go back in the café. Call the cops. Then stay inside."

Kerry stared at Carl, frozen by the car door, her mouth open, still unable to form his name.

"Don't give me any trouble now!" he screamed in a broken voice. "Just do what I said, and *don't come back*!"

She saw the sweat streaming down his face like tears. She saw Ax turn his head in order to look at Carl. She heard the familiar chuckle.

Ax said, "You know we both could still get away, Carl. Pick up our cut. We can still bargain."

Carl pushed the gun against Ax's head, hard. "Shut

up, Ax! Keep your hands on top of your head!"

"Listen, kid," the soft voice said, "if you talk, you won't last two minutes in any prison system they've got."

"Kerry!" Carl screamed at her. "For God's sake, *move!*"

Stumbling blindly, Kerry turned and fled up the steps to the café.

Jeff sat tensely beside Detective Potts in the car the deputy was driving. Sheriff Brightwell was in the front giving instructions to the other department cars behind them, talking to the small city force by radio, keeping their cars under his command.

Jeff saw the blue Chevy still parked in front of the bus station. "That's it!" he said.

"Block it," the sheriff ordered. "The others will deploy in the street. Hold your fire."

"Stay in the car," Potts told Jeff.

Even before they stopped, Potts had opened the door and hit the street, service revolver at the ready. Jeff saw the street blurring with men as they cautiously approached the blue car, moving closer from the protection of one official car to another, crouching, slinking toward the Chevy.

"Freeze!" the sheriff ordered. "You—throw out your weapon!"

Jeff heard the clank of metal on pavement. "That's mine," a broken voice said. "But he's got two."

The sheriff leveled his gun at the man with the scar. The rest of the team surrounded the car.

"Out!" Brightwell ordered. "With your hands on your heads. Both of you."

They got out of the car, the ugly little man and the big kid with blond hair. The sheriff ordered them to spread-eagle against the hood. They looked utterly defenseless with their hands on top of their heads while they were searched.

Potts was back at the car. "All right, Jeff, you come with me and Officer Hart. We're going in the café."

Jeff's feet were numb as he got out of the car.

"Walk in with me," Potts said. "Jeff, you spot her, but don't speak. Let me go first. You stand well behind."

Jeff's hands were wet as Potts pulled the door open and they went inside. "Cover us," Potts told the officer.

Kerry was at the counter with the cashier. Jeff was shocked at the sight of her.

"There," he said quietly.

"Get behind me," Potts ordered. "And stay there."

Jeff watched Potts move with incredible speed toward the white-faced girl.

"Kerry Blake?" he said.

Kerry's white face was turned toward them. Jeff saw her look at the badge in Potts's hand.

"We're the police," Potts said.

Her face was drained of comprehension.

"Honey," the cashier explained, "you're safe now. It's the police."

But Kerry seemed too stunned to respond.

"Jeff," Potts said, gently, "tell her."

Jeff stepped forward. Kerry stared at him blankly.

"Kerry—" Jeff said. "Kerry—it's me. Jeff."

He watched his words slowly sinking in. She stumbled toward him, and he opened his arms, catching her. He felt her shaking all over.

"It's okay," he said over and over. "It's okay. We've come to take you home."

Sandra knew she was crying into the telephone and that she was repeating herself. "Allen, she's safe! She's safe!"

"Tony told me," she heard him say.

"They're flying her home! Everything's over!" She wiped her eyes and reached for another Kleenex. "She's coming home!" she said again.

"Sandra, do you want me to come over?"

"Yes, Allen—please! I want you to come over!"

22

Kerry still seemed too stunned on the flight back to Blanton from Eagleton to take in very much of what was going on. Jeff ached for her as she gave her hesitant, halting answers to the questions Detective Potts put to her. For Jeff, too, the whole proceedings had taken on such unreality that it was hard for him to realize that it was over—that Kerry was actually safe at last and that they were on their way home.

He was aware of the scratch of the detective's pencil as he noted Kerry's answers, saw him add the small piece of cardboard with the words *The Mantle* on it to the rest of the items carefully put in envelopes and entered in the leather case Potts carried. In that case, too, Jeff knew, were the notes Potts had made of his preliminary interrogation of Carl. Ax had refused to answer questions.

Then the small plane touched down in Blanton and taxied to a spot near the terminal. Jeff saw photographers and reporters jockeying for position as they got off the plane, and he watched Kerry as she tried to get past them, Potts pushing his way through them, protecting her, guiding her to her mother. When he saw Kerry folded in her mother's arms, Jeff had to look away because his eyes were filling with tears. Mr. Davidson would drive them back to their apartment, where Kerry could clean up and rest before Potts called on her to give further instructions.

Suddenly Jeff didn't want to let her out of his sight. But Potts was saying, "Okay, Jeff. I'll take you home now. But stick close because I'd like to talk to both you and Kerry as soon as I can. I'll be giving you a call."

"Yes, sir." Then Jeff said, "I guess you'll be going back out to the Hopper House—to see if you can find what Benny was after."

Potts smiled. "I see you've learned not to put things in the form of a question. Yes. I'll see if I can make anything out of 'The Mantle.' It's bound to fit in somewhere. And that's all I'm going to say about it."

When the car pulled to a stop in front of Jeff's home, Potts looked squarely at him. "The only other thing I'm going to say is this: You are in possession of privileged information now, Jeff, and you're not to talk about it. To *anyone*. Until we have exhausted all the leads on this—to

Benny, to Ax, to Carl, to the drugs—no talking. To *anyone*. Is that clear?"

"Yes, sir," Jeff answered.

"Any leaks about any of this now could blow everything up. We must continue to work very cautiously and very quietly, giving the FBI and the Georgia bureau our full cooperation."

There was a pause. Then Potts said, "Because Kerry may not be out of this yet, Jeff. If this operation is as big as I suspect it is, a whole lot of people out there know by now that she's back home and ready to talk. They don't know how much she knows or what Carl might have told her. When I pick you up later, I'll explain all this to both of you, so there will be no mistaking the seriousness of it. Clear?"

"Yes, sir."

"Okay, Jeff. Stick close and you'll be hearing from me."

Jeff opened the car door and got out. Then Potts added, "You did a good job, Jeff. You were just right."

Jeff swallowed hard, because the words he had wanted so much to hear had finally been said. He waved, then headed up to his own front door—the familiar door he had not seen for what seemed like a century.

Kerry stood under the hot shower, soaping and rinsing her body and hair over and over until the bathroom was a pocket of steam and the hot water was gone.

It was hard for her to believe that she was really home. The flight from the small airstrip near Eagleton was a blur, the landing in Blanton an agony of trying to get past the reporters to her mother. And, mixed with all that, miserable, anxious thoughts of Carl—questions she wanted to ask the detective, but couldn't find words for.

And it was only now that the presence of the man Allen Davidson, waiting there with her mother, had registered—only now that he came into clear focus. Kerry had seen him for the first time as a shield against the reporters, efficiently friendly, as if he knew them all, yet with a firmness in his easy manner that let them know there was a limit to their questions, that the interview would not become too personal or go beyond the special bounds of necessity or legal prohibitions.

And she was aware, too, of more than just his efficiency. He had stood like a bulwark beside her mother. Somewhere at the edges of Kerry's weariness little questions began to prickle, little worries and confusions she was too tired to think about or sort out just yet.

Now, dressed in clean clothes and wrapped in a warm quilt, Kerry sat on the living room couch beside her mother to face the detective again. Jeff was there too. She blinked her eyes to make her tired brain function, peered through black spots, then brown spots, and only half heard what Detective Potts was saying.

She heard him say something like "I know you're tired and we won't stay long. But I will need you at headquarters tomorrow when we'll get your full, formal statement.

"What I want to say now is that we will want you to be very careful, Kerry. We are going to keep the round-the-clock surveillance on this apartment. We are also assigning undercover agents to you. That means one or more of our people will be keeping a close watch over you.

"We don't want you to talk to anybody about your experience. Do you understand how important this is, Kerry?"

She tried to concentrate on what he was saying, but she was so very tired. She said, "But I'm home now."

"Yes," Potts said. "Thank heaven for that. But this case is far from over, and until we tell you otherwise, you must not discuss anything that happened, anything you heard or saw with anyone. Do you understand, Kerry?"

He seemed to be waiting, so Kerry nodded slowly.

"I'll make one exception," Potts said, gently. "You can talk to Jeff."

Kerry's head was aching. She heard Jeff and the detective moving to the door. Potts was saying good-bye, that he would go over all of this with her tomorrow when she was fresh.

"Oh, wait," she thought.

"Carl—" Kerry's voice sounded small and far away to her, as if she hadn't spoken in years. "What will happen to Carl?"

"He'll have to answer some questions there in Tennessee," Potts said. "Then he'll be extradited here for questioning. If Carl will cooperate with us fully, I think we can see that he gets a sympathetic hearing. But I can't make any promises. It depends on a great many things."

Kerry nodded. She wanted to say something more, but

the words would not come. How could she explain about Carl? About how he got mixed up in all this? About how mixed up in himself he was?

Potts said, "We'll talk tomorrow. Now you need to get some rest."

When they were gone, Kerry curled up with her head in her mother's lap. There were too many things to say, too many raw places to touch so soon, but they were close here in the little apartment. Sandra stroked Kerry's hair the way she used to when Kerry was a little girl. It was like this—so long ago—when both of her parents were there to soothe her hurts. And for such a long time after her father's death, Sandra had seemed to have no reserve left over to offer Kerry, no way to give of herself when Kerry needed it. But now . . .

"Mom . . ." Kerry said, "about Mr. Davidson . . ."

Sandra went on smoothing her hair. "He's a friend, honey. A very special friend. I met him the very day you disappeared—on an assignment for Natalie. Allen is a good friend of Chief Perez's and a special member of the police force. He was very helpful—very considerate and kind—while you were missing."

"Oh," Kerry said. But she knew there was more. She knew her mother would tell her later. Somehow she didn't want to hear about it now. She wanted her mother all to herself.

Kerry looked up at Sandra. "I'm home, Mom," she said. "I'm really home."

"Yes, baby," her mother answered. "You're really home."

Kerry's eyes grew enormously heavy. The weariness was in every cell of her body. With her head cradled in her mother's warm lap, she closed her eyes. And she slept.

Jeff was aware of a change in Kerry. She had always been quiet and reserved, but he missed the sudden warmth of her shy grin. He saw less of the sparkle that was such a basic part of her before, even though it had always come at unexpected little moments. He was glad the police had forbidden her to ride her bike until they felt she was out of danger, glad that they were being careful of her, and glad, too, that it gave him the chance to pick her up after basketball practice. For once his brother didn't give him any hassle about borrowing his car, and Jeff looked forward to the time it gave him alone with Kerry.

He hadn't realized how deep the change was at first. They sometimes stopped off at McDonald's on their way home for a shake or something, and he just thought she was tired, or maybe practice hadn't gone well.

But one day they were sitting there in the privacy of the car and she said, "Jeff, sometimes I just get so down I don't know what to do."

Her voice was funny. It had such a sad, lost sound to it that he didn't know what to say.

She went on, "I—well—I just get this awful feeling that nothing is ever going to be the same again." Then she looked at him quickly. "The kids at school have been great, especially the team. I think coach talked to them and told them I might have sort of a hard time getting back in the swing of things, but I just want to be able to look them in the eye when some of the ones that don't really know me ask perfectly innocent questions—I just want to feel normal. I can't get used to undercover people following me. I don't like feeling suspicious—afraid to be alone." She stopped and looked down at her hands in her lap.

Jeff didn't want to say something silly like "Everything's going to be okay," when he didn't know himself if they would ever solve all the pieces of Ax and Benny and Carl and drugs and the stuff they had found in the ashpit of the Hopper House.

He had thought Kerry would be particularly interested in the article he'd seen in the paper. The police had found a large sack of jewels in the ashpit—about halfway down to the basement. It had been dropped in there from the fireplace of the main drawing room.

The article didn't mention anything about where they might have come from, but Jeff was sure it must have been Benny's stash. He was sure it was what Benny had meant when he scrawled *The Mantle* on the match cover he had given Carl at the gravel pit. And from the estimated value of the gems, it would be a stash that Ax would want to get his hands on badly enough to take the kinds of chances he had taken.

But Kerry had just nodded. "It's things like that, Jeff. They're not going to go away or ever end." There was a long pause, then she said, "And sometimes, even at home, I feel so uncomfortable. I get so uptight when Mr.

Davidson is around. I don't know how to talk to him or what to do, so I just say hi and go to my room."

"Well, have you ever just *tried* talking to him? About how you feel?"

"You mean how I feel about him and Mom? What's to say? I already know he's crazy about her, and she likes him a lot. But I can't tell him I don't ever want anybody to try to be my father."

"I don't mean that," Jeff said. "I mean talking to him about these other things that are bothering you. Besides, I don't think he wants to be your father. He knows how you feel about your own father. The guy thinks your mother is a very great person, and so do I. And I happen to think Mr. Davidson is one heck of a great person too. I think he would like to be friends."

"He wants to marry her."

"Well, maybe, just maybe your mother might like a really nice guy for a husband. Kerry, she knows he's not going to take your father's place with her, any more than he is with you."

She was silent.

"Well," Jeff said, "I'll tell you something about Allen Davidson that maybe you didn't know. He is doing everything he can to see if he can help Carl come out of this okay. He's gone to Jesup. He's talked to everybody from Carl's parents to his teachers and his friends."

Kerry looked at him. "How do you know?"

"Because Detective Potts said Davidson is one of the best legmen that ever helped the force out. And he helped every way he knew how to get you back. He wants to see that Carl gets every legal break coming to him. He knows what Carl did for you. And he *cares*."

"You mean that you've talked about all this with Detective Potts?"

It was then Jeff finally told her what he had held back for such a long time: He had applied for the Blanton police cadet program. The longing to share all this with Kerry had been so long suppressed by his concern for her that once he started talking, he couldn't stop. Only now could he say, at last, that Potts himself had recommended that he be accepted.

Kerry listened through it all, and when he was finished, he was nearly out of breath. She was pleased for him, he knew, and she said so. But the excitement he felt himself and hoped she would share seemed far, far away from her.

He tried talking to her about the plans for the Hopper House. This, he knew, usually caught her interest. They both were pleased that things were really coming along. Committees had been set up and they had already had a lot of planning sessions and work groups. But Jeff felt even all of this was slipping past Kerry.

It was the afternoon that he took her with him to hand out fliers all over town, telling about the first big money-making project to be held on the grounds of the estate, that he learned what was really eating at her.

They drove out the familiar route to the old mansion. The lane had been scraped and graded and had new gravel topping.

Jeff parked down in the lane, and he and Kerry

walked up the long, curving driveway together. Kerry slowed down for a minute as she studied the house.

"It's—it's so different," she said.

Jeff nodded and waited.

"It—that day seems so long ago." She stopped, but he knew what she meant. "And yet, it's just right here with me. Inside me still. The van was back there—"

Then suddenly Kerry moved away from him and leaned her head against a tree. She was crying. No sound. Just big tears tumbling from wide-open eyes down her cheeks.

"Kerry?" Jeff asked softly. "What is it? What is it *really*?"

She closed her eyes. "It's Carl," she said. "I can't get him out of my mind."

Jeff swallowed and waited, but she didn't say anything.

Then he asked, "Would you ever want to see him again?"

"How? There's no way I could ever see him. You know that."

"Yes, you could see him. Potts told me. He's being extradited, and Potts can arrange it. If that's what you really want."

Kerry looked at Jeff for a long time with the tears still streaming down her cheeks. Then she put her arms around his neck and hugged him tight. Finally she moved away and blew her nose.

He said, "I guess we'd better get you home now. It's getting pretty late."

But when he stopped in her driveway, before she could get out, he took her face in his hands and turned it toward him. Then he kissed her for the first time. A gentle, simple, tender little kiss that nearly tore him apart.

23

Finally the day came when Carl was extradited. Detective Potts arranged a visitor's pass for Kerry. He drove her and Jeff to the maximum-security facility where Carl was being held.

All day Kerry had thought of nothing but seeing Carl again. She wanted to plan what she was going to say, but her feelings were so overpowering that she couldn't.

The car stopped outside the prison.

Jeff asked, "Will you be okay?"

She nodded. "This is just something I'd like to do alone."

Kerry and Potts got out of the car. Kerry stood a moment before the gray building. She had never been inside a prison before and now she felt a coldness come over her, a feeling of approaching something so foreign that she was not sure what she should do, what she could expect.

At the door she showed the guard her pass and, with a word from Potts, she was cleared for entrance. Then Potts left her and went back to the car with Jeff.

She was told to go to the end of the hall and wait. The place was like a lost part of a nightmare, the part you can't remember although it was that part that woke you up. The huge gatelike door was pushed open with amazing speed by an unseen mechanism to reveal an enormous room.

There were no windows in that room. At its center was another guard in a small bulletproof glass tower. Guns were positioned at all angles from it. Along the sides of the room were thick glass walls.

"Your area is number 19." The guard's voice was hollow over the loudspeaker.

Kerry saw the number above a section of glass wall and moved over there. All she could see was her reflection and she waited.

At last a harsh light came on, and she could see into a small area behind the glass, and there was Carl, standing just inches away from her, and yet in another lifetime. He lifted a phone and nodded for her to do the same. She hadn't seen the phone on the hook beneath the 19.

He said, "Hello, Kerry."

"Carl—can you hear me?"

"Yes. And so can the guards."

She could feel her eyes burning with something like tears that had no place in here.

"How did you get a pass?" he asked.

"Detective Potts arranged it."

"Oh." There was a long pause. "Why did he do that?"

"Because I asked him to."

"Why?"

"Because—I just wanted to come, that's all. I wanted to see you. I—I just wanted to tell you not to give up on yourself."

He didn't say anything, so she added, "That's what I really came for."

"You've got two more minutes," he said. "Say something else."

She bit her lip. "Allen—Mr. Davidson—he's a friend of my mother's, and he's on the city council and does police work, and he's trying to help you."

"Help me what?"

"Help you get untangled from this mess."

She didn't like the way he laughed. Short, without humor. "Try something else," he said.

Kerry blinked. "I got my bike back."

"Okay. That's good."

"Oh, please, God," she thought, "give me something to say! Something that will reach him, something he can hang on to." But what was there, really? That he saved her life? He knew that. But was there anything she could do about Carl? Or that Allen Davidson could do either? Maybe it was wrong to give him that kind of hope. Maybe the worst wrong was coming in the first place.

"You've got one more minute to go," he said. "Say something else."

"Carl—" she began haltingly, "Carl—sometimes you have a feeling for one person you will never have for anyone else. *Ever.* I think that is what I really came to tell you."

The bewildered, confused look in his eyes was familiar to her now. "And you have that feeling?" he asked.

"Yes."

There was a hollow silence in the huge room. Then he said, "Thanks. Thanks. I think I know what you mean."

She placed her hand flat against the thick, cold glass. He looked at it. Then he looked at her, a look that held so many things that Kerry wanted to close her eyes. Then she saw the tight white line of his mouth as he slowly pressed his hand against the opposite side of the pane, matching her hand, finger for finger.

Suddenly the light went out in area 19, and she was left with nothing but her reflection again and the cold feeling that spread from her hand on the glass throughout her whole body. She couldn't even hear him being led away. It was like a death.

In the car beside Jeff she held herself rigid against the tears. Potts said nothing, but Jeff talked fast, and neither of them knew how to mend her hurt. Kerry heard herself say yes, and yes, and yes, and Jeff didn't seem to care if her answers didn't fit what he was saying.

Only half of Kerry was listening. The other part of her was turned back to everything she had gone through. It was this that filled her with such ineffable sadness because she could still see Carl's face as he talked to her from behind the shield of bulletproof glass.

Yes, the Hopper House would be good for other kids. But for Carl there would have to be something else. This kind of thing came too late for him. He would have to find something else to help him grow. Maybe it was there, in the system he had just been absorbed into, in prison and the rehabilitation program. But that was the same system that had produced the Axes and Bennys and she wondered.

Maybe there, just like everywhere else, it was what you chose to get out of it that made a difference. And she could only hope that Carl would choose what was right for him. Maybe it wasn't too late for him after all. Maybe he would be okay.

Suddenly Kerry realized that Jeff had stopped talking. He sat straight and still beside her now, staring ahead. Even though he had not moved away, she felt a distance between them, felt his sense of failure after his efforts to reach her.

She looked at him, but he did not turn. She could feel the gulf and a new, a different kind of loneliness began to take hold of her. She did not want this separation, this loneliness. Not for either of them.

She continued to look at him, but Jeff would not turn his head. Gentle Jeff, her best friend in all the world.

She slipped her hand into his. She could feel the warmth of his fingers close slowly over hers. Holding tight to Jeff's hand, she leaned her head back against the seat and closed her eyes.

About the Author

Janet Allais Stegeman grew up on a farm near Wheeling, Illinois, before moving with her family to Atlanta, Georgia, and then to Cincinnati, Ohio. She has worked as a medical researcher and also as a volunteer in special education classes and with the Department of Offender Rehabilitation Community-based Services. She has written articles and short stories for various regional publications, including *The Georgia Review* and *The Atlanta Journal and Constitution*.

Ms. Stegeman currently resides in Athens, Georgia, with her physician husband.